THE WOMANSLEUTH ANTHOLOGY

THE WOMANSLEUTH ANTHOLOGY:

CONTEMPORARY MYSTERY STORIES BY WOMEN

EDITED BY IRENE ZAHAVA

 THE CROSSING PRESS / Freedom, California 95019

Library of Congress Cataloging-in-Publication Data

The Womansleuth anthology : contemporary mystery stories by women
    edited by Irene Zahava.
        p.cm.
        ISBN 0-89594-272-0 : $22.95. ISBN 0-89594-271-2 (pbk.) : $8.95
        1. Detective and mystery stories, American--Women authors.
    2. Women detectives--Fiction. I. Zahava, Irene.
    PS648.D4W56 1988
813' .0872' 089287--dc19   88-443
                                                                 CIP

Dedicated to Michele B. Slung
whose book, *Crime On Her Mind:
Fifteen Stories of Female Sleuths
From the Victorian Era to the
Forties*, got me started on my search
for women sleuths.

Contents

Editor's Preface

IRENE ZAHAVA

When a new crop of mystery writers appears on the scene, it's cause for celebration. And when that crop includes women writers—writing about women detectives—then it's *really* something to notice.

In recent years, we've seen a welcome increase in the publication of mystery fiction that realistically reflects the lives of contemporary women, and places women detectives in the forefront of the genre. Characters such as Cordelia Gray, Kate Fansler, Anna Lee, Norah Mulchaney, V. I. Warshawski, Kinsey Millhone, and many others, have broken away from the macho mold which categorized American detective writing for so long. The heroines in this ground-breaking anthology proudly join forces with their female predecessors.

The fictional sleuths you are about to meet run the gamut from professionally-trained policewomen and private investigators to amateurs who stumble into crime-solving. They vary in age, background and experience but, at the same time, they have a lot in common: they are brave, intelligent, observant, quick-witted and quick-acting. They're just the sort of women you can depend on when the going gets rough.

Gertrude Stein and **Alice Toklas** team up to solve a real-life case that rocked Paris in the 1920s.

Abby Benson, queen of disguises in the N.Y.P.D., is called upon to protect a naive TV newscaster determined to explore the dark side of the New York City subway system.

Dana Sloan, investigative reporter, looks into accusations of graft at city hall. Now she's no longer worried about meeting deadlines . . . she's worried about staying alive.

Amelia Crater, gossip columnist for the *L.A. Times*, solves the mystery surrounding the death of a much-hated Hollywood agent, and for once she knows how to keep a secret.

Emma Mackey, acting sheriff of Carlton Corners, proves that a seemingly-peaceful farm community is hiding a lot of unpleasant, and dangerous, secrets.

Ivy Middaugh and **Judith Perino**, a mother/daughter detective team, don leotards and tights to go undercover in a health spa, where murder mixes with aerobics.

Anna, the housekeeper for a wealthy businessman, easily takes on the role of avenger the day her boss is murdered.

Thelma Ade, owner of Ade Detective Agency, helps the police solve a case involving the death of a soap opera star without ever leaving her office.

Colleen Bristow, who has been deaf since the age of nine, uses her lip-reading skills to help the police solve a major drug case.

Wiggins, a cool private-eye who works the L.A. scene, develops a weakness for one of her female clients, and things immediately begin to heat up.

Christine Craighton, on vacation in Cape Cod, overhears two men planning a murder. She's determined to stop them, but first she has to discover the identity of their intended victim.

Emma Twiggs, the septuagenarian aunt of a private investigator, solves the riddle of a missing diamond necklace and puts her famous nephew to shame.

I.Z.

The Adventure of the Perpetual Husbands

ELLEN DEARMORE

*I*t was hard that fall of 1921, I remember, not to get interested in the Landru case. It was all everyone was talking about. "The Bluebeard of Paris," they were calling Henri Désiré Landru, because he had had so many wives and had murdered them all except one. And of course there were his lovers; all Paris knew of them. I would go into my favorite butcher shop, up on the rue de l'Odeon, and Monsieur Renard would greet me.

"Good morning, Mademoiselle Al-leece," he would say. "We have some nice tongue today. And what do you think of Landru? Two hundred eighty-three lovers! What a man! French to be sure!"

I did not like tongue and I did not like Landru and I most certainly did not like all those lovers. So I would say, "Monsieur Renard, the quality of your meat has fallen off since you became interested in the Landru case."

"Oh, no, Mademoiselle Al-leece," he would assure me. "I will not allow that!"

But, of course, he did.

All Paris did.

Gertrude was no exception.

Gertrude, of course, loved to read murder mysteries—sometimes as many as three a week. She also liked to think of herself as a detective. "It's the perfect crime," she said. "He murdered eleven people, and yet not one body has been found! What did he do with the bodies?"

The newspaper *Le Monde*, I remember, was asking the same question, and offering 5000 francs for the best answer.

"I have never won 5000 francs before," Gertrude said. "That would take us quite nicely to the south of France next summer. With that much money we could even stay through the fall. It's definitely worth my time."

So all of Paris went mad over Landru and Gertrude went mad over Landru and then finally, I am sorry to say, I did too. The day I found out about the *petite annonce*.

Four years earlier, in 1917, the year that Gertrude had bought her first Ford car and learned how to drive, Gertrude and I had been helping out in the war effort. We were working for the American Fund for the French Wounded, delivering hospital supplies to a number of French cities. We were in and out of Paris all that year, first down to Perpignam, than back to Paris, and then on to Nîmes. But before we went to Nîmes I decided to get rid of the heavy old Smith Premier typewriter that I had been using for years. So I placed a *petite annonce* in the newspaper.

I remember my advertisement quite well. *For Sale: Smith Premier typewriter, excellent condition. Contact Alice Toklas, 27, rue de Fleurus, 6e.* It was during the war when people still trusted one another and thought nothing of placing a *petite annonce* in the newspaper, even mentioning their names and the fact that they were women, although after the war and the Landru case they thought twice about doing such a thing. But I placed my advertisement in the paper and several people came by and inquired about the typewriter. But none of them bought it. One thought it was too heavy and old—which it was—that's why I was trying to get rid of it. Another wanted a French typewriter with the cedilla and the circumflex and the Smith Premier was an English typewriter. I began to realize that selling this typewriter was going to take some time, and Gertrude and I didn't have much time then. So I withdrew the advertisement, put the Smith Premier back into the closet, and thought no more about it. Until the day four years later when Gertrude reminded me.

"Alice!" Gertrude came into the kitchen one afternoon, early in the case, while I was preparing dinner. She was obviously excited and out of breath and had a newspaper in her hand.

"Listen to this," she said, opening the newspaper. "It's about Landru."

2

"It is by now quite clear that the way this most monstrous of murderers met his victims was through the means of the petite annonce. The unsuspecting woman would place her small classified in the newspaper, sometimes offering for sale items of jewelry or clothing, sometimes pieces of furniture. Answering her advertisement, presenting himself at her door, would be the pleasant, smiling, polite, soft-spoken, always confident Landru, ready to make an offer all the more liberal than the woman was asking, since his intention was to pay in other than cash. And how could these honest, but guileless starved-for-affection, middle-aged women know that this man who had suddenly appeared so innocently on their doorsteps, who was to flatter them and court them and who would marry ten of them, how could they know that it would be he who would take them on the darkest journey of all, to a death more horrible than any of them could imagine?"

Gertrude looked up from the paper.

"Do you remember, during the war, when you were trying to sell the Smith Premier? You placed a *petite annonce* in the paper."

"I remember."

"What year was that?"

"Nineteen-seventeen. The year you bought the Ford."

"I thought so. Who answered the ad?"

"Three people—two men and a woman."

"Did either of the men have a beard?"

"No."

"Are you sure?"

"I always remember a beard."

"Then it wasn't Landru," Gertrude said, laying her paper down. "That's a relief! But don't you see how close you came? That's the way Landru met his victims—through the *petite annonce*. Nineteen-seventeen was his busiest year—he met and murdered five of his victims then. Don't you see? Landru could have come to this very house! One of the things he bought from one of the women he murdered was a *typewriter!*"

Gertrude looked at me, and I looked at her, but neither of us said another word.

That was when I became interested in the Landru case.

•

I am sure that if I had let her, Gertrude would have been content to spend the rest of her life in her chintz-covered chair by the fireplace, just thinking thoughts. I called her Sherlock Holmes on several occasions, but I could just as easily have called her Ralph Waldo Emerson or Sigmund Freud. For of all the things in the world, Gertrude loved to think most of all.

I once said this to Picasso, her closest friend for many years.

"No," he said, "you're mistaken. Gertrude likes to move best of all. I think of Gertrude always in her car, driving through the countryside."

"Don't let that fool you," I said. "She moves in order to find things to think about."

Picasso was not sure of that but I was. Of all the things in the world, Gertrude liked to think best of all. And her favorite kind of thinking was the kind I could not understand.

I once read a book about some medieval monks who were called Scholastics and who spent their lives thinking about such things as how many angels could sit on the head of a pin or how many teeth a horse had. As for myself I have never been much interested in how many angels could sit on the head of a pin. And if I needed to know how many teeth a horse had, although I can't imagine why I would ever need to know such a thing, I certainly would not think about it. I would simply go find a horse, open its mouth, and count its teeth. But Gertrude was different. Gertrude liked to think about that horse, while sitting in her chintz-covered chair, and try to imagine how many teeth it had.

I once accused Gertrude of being a Scholastic, the last of the medieval monks, and she said, "That's not true. Thinking is essential to me, it is not an intellectual game. Every thought I have is another attempt for me to understand the world. I think so that I may live. I think so that I will know who I am and by knowing who I am know who others are too. I cannot exist without thoughts."

And so Gertrude thought.

So whereas most people would have started right off with the problem at hand, the one *Le Monde* was offering 5000 francs for, the one the police had not yet been able to solve—how Landru had disposed of the bodies of his eleven victims, ten wives and the son of one of the wives—Gertrude started off with something else. What kind of crime it was.

"It's a French crime," Gertrude said to me one night after dinner as we were sitting in the atelier. "French crimes are between men and their lovers and American crimes are between fathers and their children. Lizzie Borden is an American crime and Landru is a French crime. That's too bad. I understand American crimes much better. I must think about that."

So Gertrude thought about it and then, several nights later, brought up the subject again.

"Do you remember our discussion about French crimes and American crimes?"

"Yes."

"Well, I've written something. It's called *An American Crime*. I'd like to read it to you."

Gertrude began.

"An American Crime

> Lizzie Borden took an axe
> And gave her Mother forty whacks
> When she saw what she had done
> She gave her Father forty-one

I have thought about it often, that rhyme.
And who wrote it.

Some say a man wrote it and some say a woman wrote it but no one knows for sure.

It may be the most important part about the whole thing, that rhyme and who wrote it, surpassed only by the fact that Lizzie Borden was guilty but not in the eyes of a jury only in the eyes of God.

There is guilt and there is guilt, big guilt and little guilt and the question becomes who does the big guilt belong to and who does the little guilt belong to.

Some say the big guilt belongs to fathers and mothers but especially to fathers and I do not disagree. And some say the little guilt belongs to sons and daughters but most especially to daughters as they have fathers while sons mostly have mothers. And I do not disagree.

5

So there is big guilt and little guilt and fathers and daughters and mothers and sons but mostly fathers and daughters.

And daughters.

And daughters must be daughters until they marry or until their fathers die at which time they can become women. This in some respects is as difficult as being a daughter only not as difficult because you no longer have a father. Only some women even when they are women are still daughters so much did they have fathers. So it is difficult being a woman but it is more difficult being a daughter.

I know.

And by now I also know something else.

About that rhyme.

Who wrote it.

Most certainly a daughter."

Gertrude finished reading and then looked up.

"Do you understand what I am saying?"

"You are writing about your father. And yourself. And, of course, the fact that Lizzie's father got one more whack than her mother. It's a nice piece, Gertrude, and I'm glad you wrote it. But I don't see what it has to do with the Landru case."

"It has nothing to do with the Landru case," Gertrude said, raising her voice. "But it was important for me to have that thought. Now I know about American crimes."

●

Somewhere early in the case Gertrude began keeping a file on Landru. She would go out once a day, sometimes even more, when the events of the trial had been especially sensational, and buy the latest newspaper accounts. I also remember the cheap pamphlets that were sold on the street. There was a biography of the one wife, Fernande Segret, who had somehow managed not to be murdered, although Landru had taken her out to the villa at Gambais where he had killed the others. She was only eighteen years old, and so the pamphlet was not very long. But it did, according to Gertrude, shed some light on the case. So bit by bit Gertrude began to put together a file on the Landru case.

"I've made a list," Gertrude said one night, as we were sitting in the studio," of some of the things I want to think about in the Landru case. I must see it in words—if I am going to solve it."

Gertrude began reading from her list.

"Number One: the fact that Landru had 283 lovers.

"He had ten wives, too, but he also had 283 lovers. That may be the most startling fact about the whole case. Can you imagine?"

"I would prefer not to try."

"It would certainly take a lot of energy."

"To say nothing of deception."

"That's one way to look at it. Another is to think that maybe he brought them some happiness, that but for him 283 women might possibly have never been loved."

"*Gertrude!* But we are talking about murder."

"Perhaps. But perhaps we are also talking about love."

"I think not."

"Maybe so."

Gertrude went on.

"Number Two: his name: Henri Désiré Landru.

"His Christian name, Henri, which turned out not to be so Christian, after all. But *Henri.* Doesn't that bring to mind Henry VIII, who had six wives and murdered two of them? To this unfortunate name of Henri was added the even more difficult name Désiré. To desire. That explains the 283 lovers. You know my theory about names: to name is to claim, to name is to blame, to name is to determine. In this case it obviously determined."

"Number Three: Landru's appearance.

"He's fifty-two years old, short—only five feet, six inches—bald, has a sallow complexion, and a long pointed beard. How then do we explain the uncanny attraction that women felt for him? There were his eyes, several of his lovers mentioned his eyes. 'Mesmerizing,' 'serpent-like,' 'charming.' But was that enough to cast such a spell? There is, of course, his car. Many of his women mention that. And there is no doubt that a car makes one more attractive to women. But does that car explain the whole attraction? Probably not."

"What's his sign?" I interrupted.

"What?"

"His astrological sign."

"Is that important?"

"It could be. It might even give us just the clue we need."

"You know I don't believe in that. We've got to stick *to the facts*, Alice."

Gertrude looked back at her list.

"Number Four: the famous death carnet.

"This notebook, of course, is the evidence that will finally send Landru to the guillotine. In it he lists the names of all his victims. The name is followed by a date, then by a time.

"For example: 27th December 1916, Madame Collomb, 4:30 a.m.

12th April 1917, Mademoiselle Babelay, at 4 a.m.

1st September, 1917, Madame Buisson, 10:15 p.m.

26th November, 1917, Madame Jaume, at 5 a.m.

"The time is the time he murdered them, but how strange to record it. There is also this inscription beside each name: 'one single, one round-trip to Gambais.' He would buy himself a round-trip train ticket to Gambais, knowing that he would return to Paris. But as he also knew the woman who was with him would not return, he would buy her only a one-way ticket. How curious, and how curious to record it."

"And how mindful of his money," I said. "He is obviously not a wasteful man."

"Number Five: the question of what Landru did with the bodies of his eleven victims.

"This is, of course, the great mystery. The police speculate that he burned parts of the bodies—the most identifiable parts, heads and such—in the kitchen stove at Gambais. A pile of ashes, presumably some of the remains, was found in the shed in the back of his house. They also found teeth and bones belonging to three women in the shed. But where are the rest of the bodies, and how did he get rid of them? That is the question everyone would like to know."

Gertrude looked up from her list.

"These are the things I would like to think about. But before I can do that, I must think about something else. The man himself. What kind of man is Henri Désiré Landru? And how does his mind work? If I can understand the way his mind works, I will know what he did with the bodies."

"It's quite simple," I said. "He's a husband."

"A *husband?* I didn't think of that. But if so, a very peculiar one."

"A perpetual one."

Gertrude laughed.

"Is that a husband then? Or is that a contradiction in terms? One can be a husband once, but can one be a husband ten different times?"

"Eleven times. Landru had one legal wife. He didn't kill her."

"Can one be a husband eleven different times? I need to know what a husband is. I think I know, but maybe I don't. I will ask Hemingway."

•

Hemingway, of course, was the other perpetual husband in this adventure—he had four different wives before he was through, although at the time when Gertrude and I first knew him he had only one, his first, Hadley.

"There are two ways of looking at that," Gertrude used to say, referring to Hemingway's wives. "Either he like marriage so much he wanted to keep experiencing it, only with a different wife each time. Or he didn't like marriage at all."

I was inclined to believe the latter.

Gertrude had just met Hemingway when this adventure took place, through her friend Sherwood Anderson. Gertrude was immediately taken with Hemingway; I was not. From the first I didn't trust him.

Most people think of Hemingway as a great boisterous man who hunted lions in Africa and fought bulls in Spain and who was afraid of nothing. But the Hemingway I knew in his early twenties was anything but that. He was so shy, in fact, that sometimes he couldn't even look me in the eye. That is because I frightened him, Gertrude used to say. But if that is so then everyone must have frightened him. Because I never saw him look anyone in the eye. Except, of course, Gertrude.

Perhaps the problem with Hemingway—of course there were several problems with Hemingway—but perhaps the first one was his wife, Hadley. Not that there was anything wrong with her. She was lovely and sweet and adored Hemingway in spite of what he later did to her and was probably doing to her all along. But the problem with Hadley was that Hemingway never brought her to the rue de Fleurus, as the other men brought their wives.

One of my jobs at the rue de Fleurus was to sit with the wives. This would free Gertrude to sit with the husbands and they would laugh and talk and have intellectual discussions while I would sit with the wives and talk about perfumes and hats and exchange recipes. I did not mind sitting with the wives. Sometimes they were interesting but most of the time they were not. But I did not mind. But the problem with Hemingway was that he never brought his wife and so I had no one to sit with. Hemingway would sit with Gertrude and they would laugh and talk, and all the time I would wonder what am I supposed to do? There is no one for me to sit with. So should I sit at all or should I just move around, pretending to sit, or should I just leave the room altogether?

There was no such problem with Picasso. When Picasso would come to visit Gertrude he would always bring Fernande and I would sit with Fernande and talk about hats and perfumes and exchange recipes, although Fernande was not much of a cook—rice was her specialty. And Gertrude would sit with Picasso and talk about art and artists. And then after a while Picasso would leave. But Hemingway never left.

So Hemingway was a husband although he didn't bring his wife and Gertrude wanted to know what that was like.

"What does it mean to be a husband?" she would ask Hemingway as they sat in the studio with their knees almost touching—although that was later, their knees almost touching. At first it was bottom on the floor, Hemingway sitting at Gertrude's feet, looking up. "I think I know, I almost know, but it is important for me to know. If I am to solve the Landru case."

"Do you want me to be frank?" I remember Hemingway asking one day. Of course Gertrude did.

"Well, then, it means that I can have sex with Hadley. Before I was married, I couldn't do that. I could have, but I didn't."

"That's quite interesting," Gertrude said. "But let me ask you this. If I were to have sex with you, Hemingway, would that make me your wife?"

"Yes, you would be, as long as we had gone through a marriage ceremony. No, wait. Can't a marriage be annulled—if the two people haven't slept together?"

"I think it can. So we would have to have sex in order to be husband and wife."

"Yes."

"Well, that gets us somewhere. But aren't there other considerations besides the legal ones? If you were my husband, for example, wouldn't that mean that you would feel some kind of emotional commitment toward me?"

"I wouldn't have to be your husband to feel that. I could feel it before we were married."

"Then we are back to the question of legality. All being a husband means is that one can, and must, have sex with one's wife."

"It looks like it."

I did not like to hear them talking this way, about what it meant to be a husband. Because I could hear the other conversation that was going on between them, the real one, and I disliked that one even more than the one they were saying out loud. That's when I started feeding Hemingway. I would go into the studio—because, of course, most of the time Hemingway was there I was in the kitchen—and would say to him, would you like some homemade plum liqueur—Hemingway loved my homemade liqueurs—or would you like a fresh scone, I have just baked them. Although I knew that I was feeding Hemingway and thus encouraging him to come again I also knew that I was keeping them from talking about what it meant to be a husband. Hemingway had that effect on some people. I have a *faiblesse* for Hemingway, a weakness, Gertrude would say. And while I most certainly did *not* have a *faiblesse* for Hemingway, I had to acknowledge him for Gertrude's sake. So I fed him scones and more scones until finally Gertrude said, "Thank you, Alice, but Hemingway has had quite enough scones."

But Hemingway was not much help with that question, I remember, about what it was like to be a husband. Of course he knew nothing about it, Gertrude was later to say, after her *faiblesse* had passed—he having never really been one. But at the time she thought Hemingway was one. He was everything, the sun, the moon, and oh, those eyes! she would say, *extraordinaire!*

"You are barking up the wrong tree," I said one day after a particularly exhausting session with Hemingway. "You are never going to get anywhere with the Landru case as long as you think it's about husbands. Landru is a husband, but the case is about wives.

"Wives?"

11

"Yes. How all those women could have fallen for such a man, how not one of them ever suspected a thing, not even his real wife, the legal one. Didn't she ever wonder why he never came home, or what he was doing all the time he was away from her? And the others—the ten that he murdered. Didn't any of them wonder what kind of work he did? He didn't have a job. Didn't any of them wonder where he got his money from? And the one who got away. What was it she said when the police came to talk to her? I would do it all over again, I love him so. See? It's about wives."

"I hadn't thought of that."

Gertrude paused.

"Are you angry?" she asked. "You sound angry."

"No, it's just. . . ."

"What?"

"Hemingway. I wish he had a home of his own."

Gertrude laughed. "He's just young. And away from home for the first time."

"First time? He came to Europe years ago."

"Hemingway's just young, and a little frightened. And no matter how old he gets, it'll always be the same. He'll still be away from home for the first time. Don't be too hard on Hemingway."

•

It was hard not to be hard on Hemingway. Because almost every day there was something else.

Early in their relationship Gertrude had decided that she would teach Hemingway how to write. "I can do it one of two ways," she told him. "Either in the abstract or the concrete. Which would you prefer?"

"The concrete," he said.

"All right, then," Gertrude answered. "Bring over some of your stories."

"Yes," she said to him one day after she had read them. "Some of them are good but most of them are bad. I will say why in a minute but first I must say this. No one writes a story, Hemingway, in which a woman complains about the size of a man's sexual organ. You can, of course, but if you do you will be one kind of writer and I don't think you want to be that kind. You must define yourself from the first."

"I was just trying to portray reality as I see it."

Or as you wish it were, I thought.

"Well, don't," Gertrude said. "It's simply not done. It's *inaccrochable*. Nobody likes to be offended when they read."

"Now, then," Gertrude continued. "Let's talk about your writing. You need to learn many things, Hemingway, so many that I don't know where to begin. Perhaps with description. You seem fond of that."

"It's my favorite kind of writing."

"That may be so. But like all beginners you have tried to put in too much. When you describe the river you once went fishing in, for example. There's so much here that I can't see the river. You must start over, and concentrate."

Hemingway began describing the river to Gertrude, concentrating, and I thought here is a safe place for me to leave, I had to run some errands. I was gone for an hour or so and when I returned I went straight to the kitchen, as was my habit, and began to prepare dinner.

I hadn't been in the kitchen five minutes when I heard laughing and scuffling coming from the studio. Uh, oh, I thought, that does not sound like description. "That's not fair, Hemingway," I heard Gertrude cry out, "it's below the belt!" What is below the belt I wondered as I started for the studio. The scuffling got louder and louder and then when I

I went back into the kitchen and started with dinner again although I must admit it was hard to concentrate on the brussel sprouts. I hadn't known that Gertrude had boxed when she was in medical school.
him I used to box when I was in medical school. We have a bet that I can't go three rounds with him. I'm winning!"

"Only because I'm letting you!"

They both dropped their gloves and looked at me.

"Don't let me interrupt anything important," I said.

Gertrude turned to Hemingway. "Put up your dukes," she said. "Or have you conceded defeat?"

Hemingway put up his dukes.

"OK, Hemingway," Gertrude said. "Prepare for a right to the jaw!"

I left the room.

I went back into the kitchen and started with dinner again although I must admit it was hard to concentrate on the brussel sprouts. I hadn't known that Gertrude had boxed when she was in medical school.

I said this to her later that night, after dinner.

"I was sure I had told you," Gertrude said. "At Johns Hopkins. I was a little overweight then and I thought the exercise would do me good. So I hired a sparring partner—Buzz Gleason. A welterweight. We boxed every night after dinner in the living room. It was when I was on East Eager Street. I've told you of East Eager Street?"

"Yes."

"But it didn't do any good, so I gave it up."

"Gertrude," I said. "I think you should tell Hemingway about us. He doesn't seem to know. I get the feeling he thinks you're available to anyone who comes along."

"That's hardly possible!" Gertrude laughed. "I'm old enough to be his mother! He's twenty-two years old!"

"That's why you should tell him."

"I can't, Alice. I don't know him well enough yet, and besides, I don't think he'd want to hear. No, we'll stay as we are. Hemingway and I need each other now. He needs to learn how to write and I need to teach him. And there's the Landru case. Perhaps later I'll tell him. But for now you'll just have to be patient about Hemingway. And you'll just have to trust me."

That was the trouble, I thought. I wasn't sure I could.

●

I remember quite well when it was that Gertrude began the second part of her investigation—the part, I might add, that she should have begun with first—what Landru had done with the bodies of his eleven victims.

"Of course," Gertrude said one night as she was going through her file, "there are several questions about the bodies. An interesting one came up at the trial today. The defense brought up the fact that no blood had ever been found anywhere at Gambais—either in the kitchen where, supposedly, Landru burned some of the bodies, or out in the shed where he cut some of them up. That one's easy to answer. I know from my medical studies that if you let a dead body set for several days, then when you cut it up it will not bleed. So that problem is solved. Now we come to the difficult part—how he got rid of the bodies once he cut them up. *If* he cut them up. We know that he burned parts of

14

them. They found one hundred kilos of ashes out in the shed. One hundred kilos—over two hundred pounds! That's a lot of ashes! How many bodies would that make?''

Gertrude thought about that for several days and then she seemed to stop thinking about it. And Hemingway didn't come around for a while and so I let my guard down and began to think that things had returned to normal.

That was my mistake.

I had been out shopping one day and returned to the rue de Fleurus around four in the afternoon. I opened the door and walked into the pavilion and knew immediately that something was wrong. I could see smoke in the hallway and I thought, the place is on fire!

I ran toward the kitchen and the smoke became thicker and there was a terrible smell and I thought what on earth is burning? Did I leave something in the oven? Then I got into the kitchen and saw that they were both there, Gertrude and Hemingway, standing next to my stove.

"Don't be alarmed," Gertrude said. "We are watching it closely."

"What on earth are you cooking?" I asked, running toward the stove. "The temperature is up to seven hundred degrees! You'll destroy my oven!"

"No," Gertrude said. "It's made of cast iron. It comes from America. It'll burn anything."

"What are you doing?"

"We're almost through," Gertrude said. "It won't be much longer. We're going to completely reduce a body to ashes, and then weigh them."

"A *body*?"

"Not a real body. A sheep's head. But the principle's the same. We've worked out a formula for converting the weight of the sheep's ashes to human bone density."

I turned to Hemingway. "*You* put her up to this!"

"No," Gertrude said. "I thought of it myself. But Hemingway's helping me. He's especially good at math."

I couldn't help it, as I stood there with my oven on fire and the smoke pouring out and Hemingway there, *in my kitchen*, I was so angry that I started to cry. There were so many tears that I finally had to leave the kitchen and go up to my bedroom. Gertrude came after me.

"Alice," she said, knocking on my door. "I'm sorry about the oven. But I'm sure we haven't destroyed it."

I didn't answer.

"Please don't be angry. We meant no harm. But it's something I must know."

I still didn't answer.

"I know how you feel about your kitchen. But it'll be the same again—as soon as it's aired."

I said nothing.

"I've asked Hemingway to leave. He's gone now."

Silence.

"I know when Landru was born," Gertrude said, changing the subject. "You asked me that once. His astrological sign."

I almost spoke, but caught myself.

"Pussy?" Gertrude said. "Please speak to me."

"Go away. I don't want to talk now."

Gertrude went away.

I sat there on the edge of the bed trying to calm myself and slowly I did. Then I thought this is the second time Landru has caused me trouble—first with my typewriter and now with my kitchen. There's only one thing left to do. I'll have to solve the case myself, and put an end to all this.

I am sick and tired of perpetual husbands!

•

The next morning while Gertrude was still asleep I went into the atelier and began going through her Landru file. I wasn't sure what I was looking for but I knew I would know when I saw it. I thumbed through the newspaper clippings, paused over a genealogical chart that traced Landru's ancestry back five generations, looked at the notes Gertrude had made along the margins of the chart, then went on. Near the bottom of the file, there was a pamphlet that caught my eye: "The Making of a Murderer: An Astrological Reading of the Mass Murderer Henri Désiré Landru." It was Landru's horoscope!

I quickly opened the pamphlet and saw there, on the first page, Landru's chart. Beneath the chart was a listing of the positions the planets had been in at the moment of Landru's birth.

Henri Désiré Landru, born 17 April 1869, 6 a.m. at
2° Latitude, 49° Longitude

Positions of Planets by Signs

Sun	22°	Aries
Moon	24°	Aries
Mercury	5°	Aries
Venus	15°	Aries
Mars	16°	Leo
Jupiter	26°	Aries
Saturn	26°	Aries
Uranus	13°	Cancer
Neptune	17°	Aries
Pluto	15°	Taurus
Ascendant	10°	Taurus

The first thing I noticed, as I looked at Landru's chart, was the large number of planets that had been in the sign of Aries when he was born. Seven of the ten planets were there—an amazing concentration! That figures, I thought. Aries are the bullies of the zodiac. Once would be enough, but to have it in your chart *seven different times!* No wonder all those women were murdered! As I continued to look at the chart I saw something even more amazing. Landru's ascendant was Taurus. My sun sign was Taurus so I knew about Taurus and I also knew that the ascendant could be as dominant a force as the sun sign itself. And if that were true and it was then I knew what that could mean.

So Landru's ascendant was Taurus.

Hmmmmm.

There was only one thing to do, I realized, as I lay the pamphlet down. Go to Gambais and check things out for myself.

Now that I knew what to look for.

●

I was taking no chances as I arose the next morning. I had suspected that Landru was an early riser. Most Tauruses are, having been born in late April or most of May when the weather starts to get nice and people want to be out of doors—just the opposite of Aquarians, who are born in the dead of winter and so never want to get up at all. But if Landru

17

was an early riser then it might be important for me to get up even earlier than he had. So I had gotten up extra early, around four, and begun to dress for my journey.

Gertrude, of course, was still asleep, having just gone to bed, and wouldn't be up until noon. I debated for a moment whether to leave her a note telling her where I was going, and then decided against it. With any luck, I would be back before noon and there would be no need to explain anything. Except, of course, the solution to the case.

I took a taxi to the Gare Montparnasse and got on the fast electric train that went to Versailles and got off halfway there at the town of Gambais. I call it a town but it was only a village, maybe not even that, just ten or twelve houses in a row along a cobblestone road. I walked through the town fairly quickly—it does not take long to pass ten houses—and I thought, where is Landru's villa? It was still very early, a little past five, and not many people were up yet. But I did manage to find one man who was delivering milk in a little cart he pushed over the cobblestones. "Landru's *villa?*" he snorted, after he had told me how to get there. "More like a broken-down pig sty."

I walked to the edge of town and started down the dirt road that led toward Landru's villa, all the time coming closer and closer to a forest that seemed to circle the edge of town. That forest was tempting to think about, with all those dark and hidden places to bury bodies in. But I thought no, forests belong to Sagittarians, not to Tauruses. I'm looking for something else.

I finally came to Landru's villa at the end of the road and saw what the milkman had meant. It was a small stone house, so small it looked more like the servant's quarters than the main house itself. The front gate was chain-locked and had a sign hanging across it: KEEP OUT, BY ORDER TO THE VERSAILLES POLICE. So much for going to the front door and looking in the windows, I thought, although it wasn't doors or windows I wanted, or even rooms. I walked around to the back of the house and saw the small shed that Gertrude had mentioned— where they had found the bones and teeth—and I thought I have seen enough here, but I have not seen it yet.

I walked back to town and walked around for another half-hour or so and found the cemetery and thought about that for a while. Then as I was walking back up the road toward the train station I saw a long line of lorries coming toward town and then turning off and going down a road. I watched them for some time. Then I walked back to town and found the local postman—by now the town was waking up—and talked to him. Then I walked back to the train station and got on the train and started back for Paris.

As the train pulled out of the station I looked at the clock above the station door. Seven forty-five, it said. It's a good thing I did get up extra early this morning, I thought, or I wouldn't have seen it.

So Landru *is* a Taurus, after all.

He, too, got up very early, in order to do his business.

●

I didn't see much of Gertrude that day. She had gotten up extra late, around two in the afternoon while I was out shopping, and by the time I had returned she was in the studio. I hadn't had time to go in and talk to her, as I usually did, having lost some of the morning hours and so having to work extra hard to make them up. It was not until dinner that we finally saw one another.

"I've been thinking about the Landru case all day," Gertrude said as we sat down to dinner.

"Oh? So have I."

"I've been thinking that perhaps I've gotten ahead of myself, that maybe I should go back to some of the earlier items on my list. My experiment with the sheep's head wasn't as successful as I had hoped."

"There's no need for that," I said. "I wanted to tell you earlier. I've solved the case."

Gertrude looked up

"What?"

"I went to Gambais this morning—while you were asleep. I know what he did with the bodies."

"You've said nothing of this to me."

"I'm saying it now."

"But now?"

"I can't tell you. But I can show you—if you'll come to Gambais. But we'll have to get up early. We've got to be there before six."

"Six? *In the morning?* You know I can't do that!"

"That's up to you."

19

"Well, I could do this. I just won't go to bed tonight. That way I won't have to get up early—if I don't go to bed."

"That's one way of looking at it."

Gertrude and I left very early the next morning for Gambais. Gertrude, of course, didn't drive at night and as it was still dark we decided to take the electric train. Once we got to the station, however, there was a brief skirmish—Gertrude didn't like to ride public conveyances. But when it became obvious that the only way she was going to get to Gambais was on one—unless, of course, she wanted to walk—the skirmish was over. We got on the train and were in Gambais by five.

At first Gertrude was excited about being in Gambais, "the scene of the crime," as she called it.

"Why didn't I think of this before?" she said. "It's so much easier to visualize it when I'm here."

But once we got out to the villa and stood before it, she began to have doubts.

"It may have been easier," she said, "not seeing it. The villa is beginning to get in the way of my thoughts. It's becoming bigger than my thoughts and so I'm not having any thoughts. Maybe we should leave."

On the way back to town Gertrude began to feel better.

"I'm beginning to have thoughts again," she said. "I need to find a lake. He probably dumped the bodies in a lake."

"You're an Aquarius and so you thought of a lake. But he didn't. He thought of something better. Come and I'll show you."

We walked back through town and reached its eastern edge and that was when I saw them again, regular as clockwork, coming down the road, the long line of lorries.

"Do you see those?" I asked Gertrude.

"Sure. Trucks."

"*Garbage* trucks," I corrected. "Making their morning run in from Paris. They start coming in each morning around six."

"Very interesting. But I've seen garbage trucks before."

"Not *these* garbage trucks. Come with me."

We started walking down the road, following the lorries. It was not a long walk but it was a dusty one and by the time Gertrude and I had reached the quarry pits we were both coughing.

"You know I don't like to cough," Gertrude said, coughing.

"It's not much farther."

We came to the quarry pits and stopped.

"These pits go back for miles," I said. "Right up to the edge of the Rambouillet Forest. For the past six years the city of Paris has been dumping some of its garbage here."

"What are you saying?"

"That Landru knew of these pits, that he knew the trucks came here early each morning and dumped tons of garbage into them, and that he brought the bodies of his victims here and threw them into the pits. What better place to put dead bodies—than in a garbage pit, where he knew they would soon be covered with tons of garbage?"

"Ummmm," Gertrude said. "It's possible. Where were you standing when you first had this idea?"

"Over there." I pointed to a promontory that jutted out over one of the pits.

Gertrude walked over to the promontory and stood on it.

"Yes," she said, "I'm beginning to see what you mean. But there are many pits. Wouldn't that have been a problem?"

"Why?"

"Surely the trucks do not get to each pit each day. Wouldn't there have been the risk that the body might not be covered up right away?"

"But didn't you say he cut the bodies up?"

"Yes—into small pieces. Of course! That would solve the problem! They'd blend in with all the other garbage and not be noticed."

"Yes."

"There's this as well," Gertrude said, stepping down off the promontory. "The smell. I like that even less than I like to cough and so we must leave soon. But the smell of this place would have kept all but the garbage men away. It's certainly not the kind of place where people would come for picnics. So Landru was safe there too. No one would be here to see him dump the bodies."

We began to walk back toward town.

"What made you think of these pits?" Gertrude asked.

"Landru's horoscope. Of course, I saw the lorries. But before I saw them I knew what I was looking for. Landru is a Taurus—or at least his ascendant is Taurus."

"You know I don't believe in that."

"Some people do. And show me a Taurus and I'll show you a garden — or in Landru's case, a garbage pit. I knew he'd try to bury the bodies somewhere — Tauruses love to dig in the earth. So I looked for some graves at the villa. Of course there weren't any — that would have been too obvious. It's the first place the police would have looked. Then I found the cemetery in town. What a clever place to bury a few extra bodies — in a place already full of them. But when I talked to the postman at Gambais, he said that the police had already checked the cemetery. In fact, all the cemeteries in the province have been checked. That was when I saw the lorries and found the pits."

"Yes," Gertrude said. "It was a very clever plan. Nearly perfect, in fact."

By the time we had gotten back to Gambais Gertrude liked Landru's plan so much that she thought we should tell someone else about it. There was no police station at Gambais. But Gertrude remembered that the Versailles Police Department had carried out the initial investigation of the case, and so we went to Versailles. Once there we found the police station and Gertrude introduced herself to the Prefect of Police.

"I am Gertrude Stein," she said, "and I have something to tell you about the Landru case."

Of course the Prefect of Police had never heard of Gertrude Stein. But I am happy to say that by the end of the day he had. He was so taken, in fact, with what she had to say that he called the Prefect of Police in Paris and they had a long talk. Then several newspaper reporters came out to Versailles and we all went back to Gambais, again in a public conveyance, but this time one about which there was no skirmish at all — a police car. Gertrude was delighted with that.

We went out to the quarry pits and Gertrude explained it all again — this time standing on the very spot where she had first gotten the idea. The story appeared in the newspapers the next day, several with pictures, which made Gertrude even happier than the police car. The next day she received a letter of commendation from the Prefect of Police at Versailles, praising her for her fine detective work, which pleased her even more. Then she wrote up her solution to the Landru case, telling how Landru had disposed of the bodies in the garbage pits, and sent it to *Le Monde*. Her entry was judged to be the best they received and so she won the prize. Again there were newspaper stories and again more photographs and, of course, a check for 5000 francs, which pleased Gertrude most of all.

"Now we can have our summer in the south of France," she said. "This is the way I have always wanted to be able to provide for you, Alice. Someday we will be rich, I promise."

So in the end everyone was happy.

Gertrude was happy because she had gotten her name in the newspapers and because the Prefect of the Versailles Police had sent her a letter of commendation and, of course, because she won the 5000 francs. Monsieur Godefroy, the chief prosecutor in the case, was happy because the jury found Landru guilty of eleven counts of murder and sentenced him to death. And all of France, except, of course, the one wife who had gotten away, was happy because there was soon to be one less murderer in their midst.

But perhaps I was the happiest of all.

For on the morning of February 22, 1922, Henri Désiré Landru was led from his prison cell at Versailles and marched out into the courtyard, where, at exactly five a.m., his head was cut off.

I, of course, being an early riser, was up at that hour. And having read of the execution time in the newspapers the day before, I noted it on the clock in the studio.

I will not say that I was smiling, as I looked at the clock, at exactly five a.m., and observed the moment of death. But I will say that I felt moment of great relief.

That now there was one less man amongst us to have 283 lovers.

And one less husband to be unfaithful to eleven wives.

And, of course, one less subject for Gertrude and Hemingway to talk about.

Fit for Felony

GERRY MADDREN

We'd had our names, Ivy Middaugh and Judith Perino, Private Detectives, on the office door for forty-three increasingly anguished days and mother and I were on the verge of throwing in the towel when our first client walked in. Even mother, who's inclined to think of celebrities in terms of Humphrey Bogart and Marlene Dietrich, recognized Carminy Grimes. Carminy was a singer-songwriter of enormous popularity, possessed of beaucoup charisma and a perpetual smile which showed off her dentist's expertise. She also knew a hot trend when she saw one. She'd invested the proceeds from her record albums into a string of health clubs and wrote a book called *Boss Bodies*, which was selling like thermal socks in Lapland. Carminy sat down, panting prettily from the long flight of stairs one has to negotiate to arrive at our threshold, threw one shapely leg over the other and opened her Gucci handbag.

"I am being systematically robbed," she said, the little five-carat bauble on her middle finger sparkling brightly against the dull green color of her money.

"Someone is depleting the till at my Toluca Lake Health Club and I want to know who it is in a hurry." She spread ten hundred-dollar bills on the desk. "Is this sufficient to retain you to make an investigation?" Mother's eyes bugged.

"It'll do for a start," I said, making no move to pick the bills up but opening the desk drawer and getting out a notebook and pen. "In what amounts is the money disappearing?"

She fingered the silver headband she wore over her short-cropped orange hair. "I'm losing between a hundred-fifty and two hundred dollars a day. Sometimes more. The obvious suspect would be our receptionist, who also acts as cashier. But Jean's been on vacation almost two weeks and the thefts have continued, even with a substitute in her place. I don't want to call in the police, at least not yet. I just want to know who it is."

"Surely," mother said, "you don't have time to oversee everything connected with your clubs yourself?"

"The Toluca Lake one I do," Carminy replied. "The rest are franchises. They carry my name but I don't run them. The Toluca Lake Club is entirely my baby." She looked at the slim gold watch on her slim wrist.

"I've got an appointment with my agent," she explained, showing lots of white teeth.

"I'd like to ask one question before you go." Mother's tone bordered on diffidence. "Why did you choose us?"

"Because you're women," Carminy answered brightly. Mother and I looked at each other and smiled.

"The Toluca Lake Club is for women only," Carminy went on, bursting our balloon. "Outside of two instructors and a clean-up crew, males are strictly off-limits. So naturally when the pair of you show up in aerobic shoes and exercise clothes it'll seem entirely normal. To all my staff and students it'll look like you just signed up for the course." She slid one of our business cards off the stack by my desk calendar, glanced at it, and tucked it away in the Gucci. "Well, ciao," she said, waving her ring-laden fingers. The door closed behind our first client and we listened to the heels of her red snakeskin shoes clicking down the stairs. Mother clapped her hands.

"Our first caper," she said, careless as usual with the slang she had affected since we'd begun this enterprise. "Now your father'll have to eat crow." Reflecting, a pensive look came over her face. "Exercise clothes. Does that mean those tight-fitting leotards that are cut clear up to your waist?"

"So what are you worried about?" I asked, scooping the hundred-dollar bills off the desk. "You'll look like a dream. Grab the yellow pages and see if you can find a store that sells that sort of thing." She plopped the hefty phone book on her desk and began to thumb through it.

"The Body Stacker," she read aloud. "Dance and exercise clothes and shoes. Reebok Charismas, high-top Nikes, New Balance 1300's. Danskins. Tights and tops." I told her it sounded like just what we needed.

Twenty minutes later mother stood in the miniscule dressing room of a Studio City shop and feigned embarrassment over the skin-tight yellow and purple outfit she had on. It's an act I let her get away with in return for her compassion regarding my idiosyncrasies. The truth is that while dad's watching his daily dose of sports on television she's apt to be doing sit-ups and leg-lifts, a few ballet positions and some yoga. She has also been known to run up the Barham Hill all the way to Lake Hollywood, which is a run even I can't duplicate without getting winded. I pulled on a red and black leotard and stared at myself critically in the triple mirror. More salads, I decided, turning my back on my reflection and hunting for my credit card.

Carminy Grimes's Toluca Lake Club sat on the apex of a triangle, one of those developer-created islands surrounded by streams of multi-colored, multi-make automobiles. Mostly, in this neighborhood, very new ones or very old models restored to their original splendor. Both the exterior and the interior of the building were mirrored. The young woman who sat at the front desk greeted us with a warm hello. She was wearing white sweat pants and a white jacket, which was opened to reveal a hot-pink T-shirt printed with Carminy Grimes's name in four-inch-high block letters. The rates and business hours of the club were posted prominently behind her. A basic three months' membership, according us unlimited entree to classes and the use of all facilities, would cost us ninety dollars each. But the receptionist, who introduced herself as Babette, told us there was a special "Me and My Friend" membership for the same period, with the bargain rate of one hundred and fifty-five dollars, a savings of twelve dollars and fifty cents apiece. I parted with two of the bills our client had given us and waited for change. Mother, who had made me stop en route at a French bakery nearby, asked Babette if she could leave her package of baguettes and croissants at the desk. The receptionist clasped her hands against her chest.

"I beg you not to," she said seriously. "I'd probably start eating them. I've lost forty pounds by not having anything but turnips and eggplant in my apartment, both of which I hate, I just don't have an ounce of will power." Mother nodded understandingly and folded the sack quickly to extinguish the tantalizing aroma of its contents.

"We have lockers," Babette said, fishing around in one of the desk drawers and coming up with a pair of padlocks tagged with their combinations. "I'm sure you'll be able to fit your package in there."

We could. Afterward, Babette gave us a tour of the place and then escorted us to the beginners' class. It was taught by Ariel Yemetz, one of the two male instructors, and Babette tipped us off that he was called Arry, rhyming with Harry. He had a young face but his forehead extended almost to the middle of his skull. His hair, what there was of it, looked like redwood shavings. He was gently bullying, insisting we all stretch a little further, lift our knees a little higher and get our heartrates accelerating. He turned on the stereo and hollered us through a stretch, bend, kick routine with such vigor and enthusiasm that stuff spilled out of his shirt pocket. Sheepishly he chased after his chapstick, a Kawasaki motorcycle key and a bottle of white-out.

It took nearly an hour, what with the warm-up, work-out and cooloff. Then Arry grabbed a towel, wiped the sweat off his face, and announced that the class was fini for the day. While the students straggled out, catching up on gossip, nutritious recipes and the latest word on tummy tucks, Arry opened a thermos and poured a red liquid into a styrofoam cup. Mother and I were almost to the door when Babette came rushing in with word of a phone call for Arry.

"I told him you were about to start another class but he said he was your lawyer. . . ." Arry got out into the corridor at the same time we did, and we saw him heading toward the phone.

Mother wanted to try the rowing machine so I experimented with the weights. Neither of us lasted long and we trudged back to the front desk to ask Babette where we could find the swimming pool.

Her chair was empty. A pair of white Adidas micropacers, soles facing toward us, protruded from underneath the desk. We pushed past the surrounding potted plants and there was Babette, twisted into an S position on the floor.

"Do you think she fainted?" mother whispered.

"I think she's dead," I said, kneeling to check the carotid artery in her neck.

•

The police came and their forensic experts weren't far behind. Mother tried to tell them what had happened. But when she began to recite her own conclusions the police lieutenant, a tall, thin man with short hair and a stingy little mustard-colored moustache, bristled.

"This isn't *Murder, She Wrote*," he growled uncharitably, "and we're not looking for any Angela Lansburys to solve the damn case."

Mother stepped back. "From here on, I'm the original clam," she said, throwing in a quote from Ellery Queen.

Other people were questioned, notes and pictures were taken. What seemed like a long time later the place was finally emptied out and Babette's white-clad body was taken away. I tried to reach Carminy via the pay phone in the locker room but had no luck. I shrugged. It would wait. Mother and I changed into our street clothes and ventured out into the parking lot where she persuaded me to have dinner at the condo dad had insisted they buy.

"It's not *that* terrible," she said, trying to convince herself rather than me. "It's got newer appliances in the kitchen than we had in the old house. And there're no cracks in the bathroom tile."

"The bathroom in the condo doesn't have tile," I reminded her as we waited at a stop sign. She turned her head away from me and looked out the window.

"Let's change the subject," she mumbled and we settled into silence for the rest of the ride.

●

Mother whipped around the skimpy kitchen, boiling water and grating cheese while I tried to remember what I was supposed to do with the greens and fresh vegetables to make a decent tossed salad. Dad wandered in during a commercial to give me a hug. Then he stepped back, frowning.

"Your mother says I have to stop calling you Judith."

"It's all right, Dad," I said, feeling about eight years old. "It's just that I'm not crazy about the name." And never was, I thought, as I kept slicing carrots into the heap of romaine.

"When I picked it out I thought it was pefect. Your grandmother and grandfather Middaugh thought it was a whiz-bang of a name. How could you not like it?"

"Oh, Dad," I said, reaching for a cucumber, "you wouldn't understand."

"I won't if you don't take the trouble to explain anything to me."

"All right." I put the unsliced half of the cucumber on the counter and turned to face him. "I want to . . . I guess you'd call it 'redesign' myself."

"I'm listening."

"I want to dump Judith Denise and all her uncertainties, her childhood insecurities and hang-ups. All her grown-up mistakes. I want to dump Judith Denise and become a new person."

He took out a filter cigarette and inserted it into his holder. "And you're telling me the name is inhibiting you?" There was a sharp edge to his voice. Critical and defensive. "Shakespeare, you know, said, 'What's in a name?'"

"But there's a lot in a name," mother chimed in. "I remember being called Poison Ivy. *Poison Ivy*," she repeated, for emphasis.

"Okay, okay," dad gave in, not so much because of our argument perhaps, but because the crowd-roar from the television set warned him he'd missed something important. Maybe a touchdown.

"Does that mean I can get the UITH scraped off the office door?" I asked when he was gone.

"As far as I'm concerned," mother said, tossing the fettuccini noodles into the steaming pot, "you're J. D. Perino from now on." About twenty minutes later she took the warmed French bread out of the oven and the three of us sat down to dinner.

"How 'bout those Giants?" dad asked, jabbing his fork into his fettuccini. "Those Redskins were lined up on third down fourteen times. Fourteen times!" Mother sighed and passed me the grated cheese. I squelched an incipient smile. Dad's recent retirement, the resulting twenty-four-hour-a-day togetherness and especially the relentlessly televised sports were what had driven mom into the private detective business. Just as three years of working as an investigator and all-around flunky for a lawyer who had the sensitivity of an armadillo had impelled me.

I was guiding a spoonful of parmesan to the pile of noodles on my plate when the phone rang. It was Carminy. She wanted us to meet her at her home in Bel Canyon right away. She had something, she said, that we had to see. I relayed the message and mother jumped up from the table so suddenly that dad's wine glass jiggled and made a pair of dime-sized Burgundy stains on the tablecloth.

"Hey," dad hollered, "where're you going?"

"I didn't have time to tell you, dear," mother said, shoving her fettucini in the fridge and submerging her flatware in the sink of sudsy water. "We got a client today. Carminy Grimes, though I doubt if you know who that is since she doesn't play any competitive sports."

The line between his graying eyebrows deepened. "Okay, so you got a client. Doesn't mean you have to rush off in the middle of dinner. Can't be that important."

"Oh, can't it?" Mother stared straight at him, a hand on one hip. "Well, it was important enough for Ms. Grimes to give us a thousand dollar retainer." She gave me a quick that'll-get-him-where-he-lives glance. "C'mon, J. D., let's put a couple of eggs in our shoes and beat it."

I revved up the Toyota pick-up and headed for the on-ramp of the Ventura Freeway east. It was a little under forty minutes before we got to the right turn-off.

"North," mother said, referring to the map we kept in the glove compartment. "We are supposed to turn north." I did and the traffic began to thin, giving us time to wonder if Carminy knew about Babette's death.

"I forgot to say anything to her about it when she called," I lamented, shaking my head at the oversight.

"Don't be so ready to climb into your sackcloth and ashes," mother advised. "Somebody from the exercise club or the police must have contacted her by now."

Close to ten minutes later my headlights picked up an impressive but tasteful sign reading Bel Canyon Estates. A few feet from there we were stopped by a guard who checked our names to make sure we were expected. Carminy's place was up on a hill and as grand looking as a one-storey house ever gets.

"It seems the thief who's been stealing my money has a conscience," she said as soon as we got inside. "I found this confession in my mailbox." Pulling a piece of paper from an envelope, she handed it to me.

"I did it. I alone am fully responsible and I rely on you to make that fact known." It was signed Ariel Yemetz. I passed the note to mother.

She yanked out her reading glasses. "I have to admit it sounds like he was the one taking your money," she said a moment later.

"That's exactly what I thought." Carminy shrugged. "I guess that solves the case."

Mother looked down at the paper again. "Kind of short as confessions go, but to the point, I guess. I wonder, Ms. Grimes, if I could use your bathroom?" Carminy pointed her in the right direction and then turned back to me.

"Lord, I need a drink," she announced, dramatically throwing her hands in the air. "I've been locked up in a soundproof recording room since one o'clock this afternoon with crazy musicians, incompetent engineers and tunnel-visioned execs. Then I race home and find that note. I haven't even had time to get out of these damned shoes," she snapped irritably, shucking the stilt-heeled pumps onto the white carpet. "Care to join me for a belt?"

I told her I'd have a small glass of white wine if she had a bottle open. Taking me into the next room where there was a bar, she got out a fancy wine glass and a bottle of Rustridge Chardonnay. But before she got her corkscrew working the soft buzz of her phone interrupted. She reached out and said hello and then went white under her heavy makeup. It had to be at least forty long seconds before she spoke again.

"Yes, yes. Of course I'm here." She covered the mouthpiece with her red-tipped fingers and asked me to wait in the next room. I left slowly, hoping to catch a word or two of the conversation, some clue to the caller who'd caused Carminy's strange reaction, but she out-waited me. In fact, once I was in the other room she put down the phone long enough to close the door between us. Mother joined me in a minute, and, after I gave her a quick run down of my exchange with Carminy during her absence, she told me that she'd seen an extension in Carminy's bedroom. I signalled to her to check that out while I applied my ear to the door in a futile attempt to hear something.

"Funny thing," mother reported when she returned. "When I picked up the phone there wasn't a dial tone, but there was nobody on the line. You get anything?"

"The damned door's oak and two inches thick." Nevertheless we stood glued to it until we heard a flurry of footsteps. We stepped back quickly but barely quickly enough, for Carminy was traveling full speed ahead.

"I'll get back to you later," she called over her shoulder, pulling a silver bag from the closet near the door and running out to the pink Ferrari in the driveway.

"She's up to no good," mother muttered, coming up behind me as I watched the Ferrari whip down the hill. We didn't take time for a conference but made tracks to the Toyota, only to discover the keys were no longer in the ignition.

"That's why there was no one on the phone," mother said. "Carminy left it off the hook long enough to make sure we couldn't follow her."

"But like all good Girl Scouts," I smiled, dragging my spare key from the zipper compartment of my satchel-like handbag, "I'm prepared." Mom gave a victory yell and we piled into the truck, fastened our seat belts and careened down the hill. I slipped through a couple of yellow lights and got onto the Ventura Freeway but the damned Ferrari was nowhere in sight.

"Obviously you took the scenic route to Carminy's bathroom," I said, clutching the steering wheel so hard my knuckles were white.

"Naturally." Mother was sitting forward, glancing surreptitiously at the arrow on the speedometer, which was arching close to the seventy mark.

"Well, what did you see? Besides the phone I mean."

"It's more what I didn't see. I didn't see a typewriter anywhere."

"Which might mean she didn't type that note over Ariel's signature."

"Strictly speaking it wasn't a note but an excerpt."

"From something longer?"

"Under a good light you could see the top edge of the paper was uneven."

"I knew there was some good reason why I went into this business with you." I changed lanes, thinking I saw the Ferrari up ahead. But I was wrong and the lane-change stuck us in a slot leading off to the Hollywood Freeway and I said a number of unladylike words which mother listened to like a student bent on getting a high mark in the subject. I ran out of steam about the same time that I found an off-ramp.

"But what about her book, *Boss Bodies?* How did our esteemed client write all two hundred and eighty-seven pages without a typewriter?" mother persisted.

"Word processor."

"I didn't see one of those either."

"Pencil."

"And Mickey Spillane was a monk," mom said, showing me what she thought of that idea.

"I suppose," I ventured, "she could have used a dictating machine à la Barbara Cartland."

"I didn't see any dictating machine." Mother looked around. "Hey, where are we going?" I was heading down Riverside when she asked the question.

"We might as well toss a coin," I said. "Either we can get back on the Ventura Freeway and try to find a pink Ferrari or we can see if she ended up at the Toluca Lake Health Club. I kind of have a feeling about the Club.

"Let's give it a shot," mother said, and my foot pressed down on the accelerator as the car swung around onto Moorpark, heading toward Pass Avenue. We streaked by the Burbank Studios, passed a line of tall palms, and turned into the Club's parking lot. The Ferrari was parked haphazardly at the rear of the building. At the sight of it I jumped out of the Toyota and ran for the back door. It was locked. The front door was also locked and I regretted that I'd never taken the time to acquire and learn how to use a set of burglar's tools. A hairpin was out of the question. I was getting something like a premonition and I didn't like it.

I told mother to take the pick-up and get to a phone, fast. Carminy wasn't there to pump iron and unless I misassessed the situation we needed the police. In the meantime I went about trying every window in the place. Since the interior was air-conditioned, the windows served no real purpose. You couldn't even see through them and spider webs attested to the fact of their uselessness. Still, I tried to open one and broke two of my longest fingernails. I was on the verge of trying to kick one in when the cleaning crew arrived. As soon as they opened the door I raced inside.

"Forget mops and brooms," I cried to the confused trio, "and look for Ariel Yemetz." Our footsteps pounded through the exercise rooms like a stamping herd. In answer to a hoarse cry I traced my way to a tiled room with a half-dozen hot tubs. A guy with the name "Gordon" stitched on the pocket of his coveralls was standing on the steps of one.

His hands were under Arry's armpits as he tried to lift the unconscious body from the steaming water. In a moment we had Arry on the floor. I was pinching his nostrils and blowing breath into his mouth when I heard the Ferrari start up. I could have broken down and wept with frustration, and would have, if my breath wasn't needed for more important matters. I kept waiting for a cough or some other sign that Ariel was going to come around but nothing was happening. One of the guys on the cleaning crew was mumbling but so softly I couldn't tell whether he was praying or swearing. As I refitted my mouth over Arry's I heard a scream and then more footsteps. Suddenly, Carminy Grimes plummeted into the room. My normally docile mother was right behind.

"I stopped her cold in the parking lot," mother boasted. "Blocked the exit with the Toyota and yanked her out of her car like I was Refrigerator Perry." Then, seeing Arry, she shoved Carminy aside and dropped down beside me.

"That's a giant-sized bump on his head," she said with a grimace. "And I guess that's not the worst of his problems, either. But don't let me interrupt you, kiddo. I'll call an ambulance and you just keep on with what you're doing." I did, and was on the verge of turning blue when Arry finally coughed up some water and sucked in his first unaided breath. The cleaning crew cheered. Mother reappeared, muttered something about the fuzz taking their sweet time showing up and began pacing restlessly. Her attention never strayed far from Carminy, who hadn't moved, perhaps afraid she might have to tangle with the mighty midget Middaugh again.

The police and ambulance sirens blended into an earsplitting duet as they neared the Club. The fast-moving paramedics, however, were first on the scene. Arry was still unconscious but he was breathing on his own when they carried him outside. As soon as the police officers turned to us, Carminy came off the wall. She rolled her eyes and tossed her head prettily in their direction.

"Well," she said, "I hope we never have another accident like that again."

"Some accident," mother grumbled, appropriating a mop from Gordon and using its handle to fish a ten-pound ankle weight off the bottom of the hot tub.

"I figure this is what made that bump on the victim's head," she said, dangling the weight in front of the older policeman's nose. "If it didn't knock him out, at least it stunned him so that Miss Grimes could push him into the hot tub and hold him under the water for what she thought was long enough to drown him." I nodded in agreement. The blue knight frowned.

"You're talking attempted murder?"

I nodded again. "If my partner and I have put the pieces of this case together right, Ariel Yemetz is the author of *Boss Bodies*, not Carminy Grimes."

"She couldn't even walk up the flight of stairs to our office without getting winded. Steps, I might add, that I can run up without panting and I'm pushing . . . ah . . . older than I look. Anyway," mother went on, overcoming her temporary loss of composure, "she sure isn't in shape to do any of the aerobic exercises detailed in the book."

"Naturally, Mr. Yemetz was less than pleased when the book came out under Carminy Grimes's name. And, like any sensible author, he hired an attorney to present his claim and seek retribution. He also wrote a letter to Carminy warning her he was bringing suit."

"The orange-haired dragon lady," mother jerked a thumb at Carminy, "didn't want to be shown up as a conniving opportunist, so earlier today she put a little something toxic into Ariel's thermos."

"Which," I broke in, "should check out with the contents in the receptionist's stomach." The cop's squint narrowed.

"If Arry, I mean Ariel, hadn't gotten a phone call he would have drunk the doctored juice and this note, cleverly cropped from Mr. Yemetz's letter to sound like a confession, would have been produced." Mother handed over the slip of paper Carminy had given us earlier. "Proving, supposedly, that he'd been stealing big bucks from the Club and was remorseful enough to do away with himself."

"As it was, Babette, who told us she was tempted to eat everything in sight, helped herself to the poisoned juice and died."

"A couple of raving maniacs!" Carminy cried, focusing her big, blue eyes suggestively on the gendarmes.

"Yeah," mom retorted indignantly, "a couple of maniacs who you hired to give credibility to your story. When Ariel called you at home tonight, and you learned he hadn't bit the dust, but was still alive, and a threat, you couldn't wait to get here and ice him before he could spill the beans." I made a rapid translation of mother's pronouncement for the policemen.

"He understands," mother insisted. "He's savvy."

"Do you understand?" I asked the older one.

"I . . . think so," he replied.

"Then cart her off to the big house," mother said and I gave her a look. She shrugged. "What's the fun of being in the detective business if you can't use the lingo?" Carminy turned and started for the corridor.

"Don't let her get away," I hollered. Gordon, over six feet if he was an inch, obediently blocked her way and she turned back and viewed us with contemptuous, diamond-hard eyes.

"Oh, for heaven's sake. I was only going to get my lipstick. I'm sure this little fiasco will draw all the newscasters and tabloid reporters in town and I'd like to look my best."

"A murder-and-a-half and she calls it a 'little fiasco,'" mother groaned. "She'll probably write more songs while she's in the jug and get them on the hit parade."

"There's no hit parade anymore," I reminded her gently.

"Whatever. Do you realize it's almost midnight? Your father'll be wondering where I am." She picked up her handbag from where it had fallen and shoved it under her arm.

"Just tell him you were solving our first case."

"Hey, that's right. And I'll tell him he can get his own breakfast tomorrow. I'm not getting up until nine . . . make that ten." She grinned. "That'll knock his socks off."

When we were finally in the pick-up heading toward the condo mother asked if I wanted to spend the night. I knew she wanted me to but I turned her down. I didn't feel at home there. I really didn't feel at home anywhere. I just wanted to go back to my apartment, have a beer, burrow under my electric blanket, and shut out, for at least eight or ten hours, all the sad and depressing things in the world.

No Witnesses

ELIZABETH BURT

"Do it after the manager closes the office and puts out the lights. And do it right—nice and clean. Make sure there are no witnesses."

I opened my eyes and stared straight up at the bright blue sky for a moment, wondering if those words were the lingering remnants of an already forgotten dream. A gull teetered high above, turning its head from side to side as it hung in the early evening breeze coming in across the channel. Higher still, a jet streaked silently eastward, a plume of white vapor snaking out behind it.

The gull uttered a shrill series of mewls and abruptly swooped down and out of sight behind the rock wall dividing the hotel's beach from the public beach where I had been sleeping. I raised my head to see what had attracted him and saw the two men standing at the end of the stone jetty.

The beach was deserted. The sunbathers, the mothers and children making sand castles, the fathers reading *Time* and *Business Week*, the teenagers playing frisbee had all disappeared, leaving me asleep there in the shadow of the stone wall with a paperback mystery novel propped under my head. I tugged at the straps on my bathing suit; I could feel the skin on my shoulders tingling from my long afternoon in the sun.

"I'll need some money now. I don't do this on credit." It was one of the men on the jetty speaking. His voice was rough, as if he had been out in too many winter storms and had a permanent sore throat.

"Half now, half later. Just make sure it gets done, or I'll come looking

37

for you." The other man's voice was lighter and he pronounced his words precisely, biting off his t's and d's the way the English do.

They were a good 150 feet away, but the wind carried their voices and I could hear every word as clearly as if they had been sitting next to me. One of the men was dressed in a tan windbreaker and slacks. He had straight dark hair and, as he turned his head slightly, I had the impression of a beard. He reached into his jacket pocket and pulled out an envelope. He handed it to the other man, who looked into the envelope and seemed to be shuffling through its contents.

"It's all there. Ten thousand dollars. But go ahead and count it. Make sure."

The man counting the money was dressed like a fisherman in blue jeans, a dark jersey and boots. His hair was a tumbled mass of iron gray curls. They both had their backs to me and I couldn't see their faces.

"Okay." It was the fisherman speaking now. "It's all here. When the job's done, you drop the rest in the mail for me, parcel post, no return address. We don't meet again."

They started to turn toward the land and I dropped back into the shadow of the wall, feigning sleep. I heard the scrape of their feet on the stones of the jetty, and then the soft squish, squish as they stepped down onto the wet sand. After a minute of silence, I cautiously opened my eyes again and slowly raised my head. The fisherman was trudging down the beach toward the lighthouse. The man who pronounced his t's and d's was heading up the grass lawn toward the hotel. He was swinging his arms and whistling.

●

Tony was sitting in a white wicker rocking chair on the porch of the Chatham Inn, *The New York Times* spread across his knees. He looked exactly as I thought the publisher of one of New England's smaller newspapers should look while vacationing on Cape Cod—relaxed but not lethargic, content but not smug. A tall glass of something cold and probably alcoholic stood on the table at his elbow. He lifted it in mock salute as I propped my bicycle against the porch rail.

"Christine. I was just beginning to wonder if I should call the Coast Guard to bring you in. Everyone else came up from the beach over an hour ago." He ran his eyes over my burning face and shoulders. "Looks like you got quite a sunburn."

"I fell asleep. . . ." I sank down on the bench in front of him and reached for his glass. It was lemonade and gin. "The strangest thing just happened."

Tony's only reaction was to raise his eyebrows. He was used to strange things happening to me.

"I overheard two men talking on the beach just now, and I swear it sounded as if they were planning on *killing* someone," I said, holding the cold glass in my hands.

Tony stopped rocking in his chair. His eyebrows abruptly dropped into a frown. "They *what?*"

"I was sleeping by the stone wall on the beach, and when I woke up, these two men were out on the jetty talking. . . ." I told him word for word what I had overheard. "The fisherman was counting out *money*, ten thousand dollars of it. And he's going to get another ten thousand after the murder."

"They didn't use the word murder, did they?"

"No, but if you had heard them the way I did, you'd think that too." The lemonade and gin was almost gone; I decided I might as well finish it off. It left a pleasant buzz in my ears and I was beginning to feel very sure of myself. On the long bike ride up the hill from the beach, I hadn't been half as convinced.

"You've never seen either of the men before? You don't know who they were?"

"No, but the man in the tan jacket was going into the hotel. Maybe he's staying there. I think we should go to the police."

Tony looked suddenly unhappy. "And tell them what? All you know is that some man is paying another man ten thousand to do some kind of job. You can't even describe the man."

He was right, of course. I could just imagine the gruff police chief we had seen at the Chatham parade last Sunday taking me seriously. If I knew who the man in the tan jacket was, at least, then I might have something to tell him.

I gave Tony my sweetest smile. Even after fifteen years of marriage, he still fell for it. "You're right, honey," I agreed. "They'd never believe me. I have an idea. Why don't we go out for dinner tonight? They say they have a French chef over at the hotel. We could go early for cocktails. . . ."

•

The William Nickerson Hotel was built on a bluff looking out toward the Monomoy Peninsula, that slender finger of shifting land that stretches southward from the eastern shore of upper Cape Cod. The peninsula serves to break the waves rolling in from the Atlantic, and the waters lapping at the beach were calm in the early evening. Later, when darkness fell, we'd be able to see the great white eye of the Chatham lighthouse as it flashed around in a 360-degree arc every ten seconds, warning passing boats of the shallow waters in the channel.

The hotel was elegant and old; according to the pamphlet on the table near the entrance, its foundations were built by William Nickerson in 1670, a decade after he bought the surrounding land from the Wampanoag Indians. It seemed to be one of the few places on the Cape where people dressed formally to dine, and I was immediately glad I had decided to wear my silk dress and heels. Tony looked uncomfortable in his jacket and tie. His idea of a vacation is hanging out on a porch somewhere in Bermuda shorts and a tennis shirt.

"Christine, do you see the man you saw on the beach?" he whispered in my ear as we slid onto two stools at the bar. The woman at the front desk had told us we could have a table for two at the second seating. We could hear the clink of tableware and glassware in the dining room, and white-coated waiters with silver trays of steaming dishes on their shoulders bustled to and fro through the swinging doors to the kitchen. My stomach growled as I caught a whiff of something delicious and undoubtedly French. The people around the bar were all strangers. There was no sign of the man with the English accent.

I shook my head. "No. Why don't you stay here and I'll walk through the dining room and take a look around. There's a terrace overlooking the beach. I'll just go out there for a minute."

I strolled through the dining room on my way to the terrace doors, trying to look casual as I scanned the faces of the diners. I hadn't ever seen any of them before.

Tony had ordered a bloody Mary for me, and it was waiting in front of my empty stool as I rejoined him at the bar.

"Any luck?"

I shook my head and chewed morosely on the stick of celery they had stuck in the drink. What if the Englishman—for I was now certain the man's accent had been British—wasn't even staying in this hotel? He could have been just passing through. The task of finding him on the Cape at the height of the tourist season suddenly seemed hopeless.

Tony put his arm around my shoulders, as if reading my mind. "Don't give up yet, the night's still young."

But it wasn't until just before we were seated in the dining room that I heard that unmistakably British voice again.

"We might as well have a drink while we're waiting, Marjorie. Why don't we sit here?"

A man and woman brushed past us and pulled out the vacant stools right next to us. I poked Tony with my elbow and stared straight ahead into the mirror behind the bar. The man sitting to my right was in his mid-thirties and had a long thin face under a neatly trimmed Van Dyke beard. The woman at his side was about twice his size. She looked to be in her late fifties. Her hair was dyed carrot-red and she wore heavy jewelry on her neck and wrists and fingers. On her left hand she was wearing a diamond ring about the size of a small golf ball. It was accompanied by a thick gold and diamond wedding band.

Her voice was high and petulant and her chin quivered as she addressed her companion. Her accent was definitely Upper East Side New York. "I don't see why you couldn't get us into the first sitting, Victor. You know how I hate waiting."

He patted her hand carefully, his fingers avoiding the heavy rings like soldiers crossing a minefield. "Yes, dear, I know. It couldn't be helped, though. They have far more people here tonight than last night. And it is Friday, you know. These beastly weekend tourists *will* come and crowd everyone else out."

He glared around the room as if challenging everyone to dare say they weren't tourists. And what was *he*, I would have liked to know, if he wasn't a tourist himself, with his snobby little English accent. I leaned against Tony and muttered under my breath: "That's him. I'd know that voice anywhere."

Tony nodded without saying anything and ordered another round of drinks. I shuddered as I heard Victor order two glasses of sherry. In my opinion, sherry before dinner was almost as hard to contemplate as murder. But then again, Marjorie looked like the kind of woman who would think drinking sherry before dinner was chic.

"Do you think I'm going to get the Picasso tomorrow?" She was playing with the diamond ring on her finger.

"As long as we're willing to keep bidding. A number of buyers are going to be at the auction—that will certainly drive up the price. How high can we go?"

"Five hundred thousand, Victor. Cash. It's in the hotel safe. I already told you that."

"That's right, you did," he murmured.

She looked at him quickly, frowning. "I'm stretched to the limit right now and the bank won't give me a penny more. Do you think it's enough? Do you think the others will outbid me? What about the man from the Met?" Her voice was worried.

He patted her hand again. "I heard he won't be making it this year. I don't think you have to worry."

I nudged Tony in the ribs and rolled my eyes meaningfully as I tried to imagine what five hundred thousand dollars would look like. Had she withdrawn it in thousand-dollar bills? Since when did auctions require cash payments?

Simpering, the hostess approached the couple. Her eyes dwelled speculatively on Victor for the length of a heartbeat, then darted to the rings on Marjorie's fingers. I could imagine her doing a quick tally of the redhead's net worth.

"Mr. and Mrs. Epsworth? Your table is ready now. Will you follow me?" She gave a kind of curtsey and led them to a table in the corner of the dining room.

Marjorie Epsworth swept across the room in her organza dress like royalty; her husband stalked at her side as if ready to beat off the rabble if it approached her. The table next to theirs, near the door to the terrace, was vacant. When it was our turn to be seated five minutes later, Tony pressed a folded ten-dollar bill into the hostess' hand and explained that I was asthmatic and he'd appreciate it if she'd give us the table by the door so I could step outside if I felt an attack coming on. The hostess gave me the quick once-over, then closed her hand over the folded bill with a tight smile. We got the table.

The chilled Vichyssoise, the Veal à la Maison, the wine and dessert

42

they brought were, no doubt, excellent. I wouldn't know. My attention was directed entirely at the conversation going on at the next table. I strained my ears shamelessly, practically falling into my plate, trying to overhear every word Marjorie and Victor Epsworth exchanged. I wished I could take notes.

The Epsworths were up from New York for the auction to be held at the Blaring estate in Hyannis the next day. I had read about the auction in the local newspaper a few days before and had commented that maybe we could pick up a few knick-knacks cheap. Tony had just raised his eyebrows and replied that he wasn't willing to sell our house in Concord just so we could buy a few knick-knacks from the Blaring estate. End of discussion. As for the Epsworths, they didn't seem to have such problems. Marjorie was holding out for the Picasso. Victor had his eye on a set of sixteenth-century porcelain figurines that he hoped to get for "fifty thousand or so." I wondered whose fifty thousand he would be using. I wondered whose ten thousand he had paid to the fisherman that afternoon.

•

"I can't stand it," I told Tony as we stood on the front steps of the hotel two hours later. The dining room was empty and the diners had departed. We had lingered over after-dinner liqueurs and had been the last to leave, watching Victor Epsworth escort his wife up the carpeted stairs. "It's obvious that he's married to her just for her money and he's going to have her bumped off. We have to do something."

Tony gazed up at the facade of the hotel. Some of the lights were still on in the guest rooms on the top floor. The hostess had just told us that some of the suites ran front to back, with balconies overlooking the terrace and the beach. "I don't know what we can do except go to the police and let them take care of it, Chris. You know there could be a perfectly innocent explanation of what you overheard. We should let them check it out."

I thought of the novel I had been reading that afternoon. The heroine was in love with the police inspector and had no trouble at all confiding her suspicions to him. But we weren't in a cosy English village where everyone knew everyone else, I wasn't a beautiful young maiden, and I definitely wasn't in love with the police chief. I didn't even know him.

And If I ever got to know him, I had the suspicion I wouldn't like him at all.

"They'll never believe me," I said.

Tony nodded his head. "You're probably right. But I don't know what else we can do."

•

"So let me get this straight, Mrs. Craighton. Just because you hear this guy saying he doesn't want any witnesses, and just because his wife happens to be loaded and twenty years older than him, you think he's going to bump her off?" the police chief asked for the second time. Up close, he didn't look any friendlier than he had last Sunday in the parade. There were bags under his eyes and a dark growth of beard on his jowls. The young policeman at the desk had warned us he would be in a bad mood if we roused him out of bed at midnight to hear some crazy story.

I nodded my head. "And there was the money."

"Did you actually see any money?"

"The fisherman was looking inside the envelope and seemed to be counting. He said it was all there. Ten thousand dollars."

Chief Nutting sighed and tipped back in his chair, scratching his chest under his wrinkled uniform shirt. He looked pointedly at the Timex clock hanging on the wall over the door. It was one o'clock in the morning.

"What did this fisherman look like?"

"I didn't see his face. He was heavy set and had curly gray hair. He had a very hoarse voice."

The chief looked at the young policeman. "You know anybody fits that description?"

"Could be Freddy Jones, Chief. He got hit in the windpipe in a fight a couple years ago. Never got his voice back again."

"He ever been in trouble with the law?" The police chief had been recruited from the Boston police department just two years ago, the young policeman had told us. He hadn't yet had time to catch up with the local lore, I decided.

"Yes, sir. In fights all the time. Did a year at Walpole for cutting up a woman pretty bad about eight years ago. It could be him."

44

"You know where he lives?"

"Down by the marina. He has a room over the boat supply shop."

The chief brought his chair down with a thump. "Okay. Call Heckler on the radio and tell him to stop by there and pick up Jones for questioning." He turned to me. "You want to wait in the other room? So you can tell me if he's the man you saw. This shouldn't take too long."

The wooden bench in the next room was hard and uncomfortable and for a while I stood examining the faces in the wanted posters on the wall. I didn't see anyone I recognized and finally settled down next to Tony. The young cop brought us a brownish liquid in styrofoam cups that he said was coffee. I wasn't sure if I could believe him but sipped it anyway. I shouldn't have believed him.

About an hour later, he told us the chief wanted us.

Nutting's jowl was a shade darker than it had been an hour before and his voice sounded like a rusty hinge scraping against an old door. "Freddy Jones is out fishing," he rasped. "We're gonna have to wait 'til he comes in tomorrow morning to talk to him. I'm not gonna bother er the Epsworths until after I see what he has to say. You can go back to your hotel and get some sleep. I'll get in touch with you in the morning if I need you."

We shambled sleepily out of the office and stood for a moment on the steps of the police station, breathing deeply. The cool night air was a relief after the stuffy air inside. A full moon was shining over the peaceful village and we heard the church clock chime two o'clock as we got into our car and drove obediently toward the Chatham Inn.

•

Chief Nutting wasn't any more cheerful the next morning when I called him at nine o'clock.

"Nah, Freddy hasn't come in yet. Don't worry, we'll talk to him as soon as he puts in to the dock."

"Aren't you going to talk to the Epsworths? She could be in danger," I insisted.

"No, ma'am, I'm not going to talk to the Epsworths. If Freddy is supposed to knock her off, like you say, he can't do anything while he's out fishing, now can he? So as long as he's out fishing, she can't be in danger, right?"

I was sure that was what they called circular reasoning back in basic philosophy, but I didn't have the heart to debate the point. Instead, I said good-bye to the chief and thumbed through the slim Cape Cod directory until I found the number for the William Nickerson Hotel.

"Mr. and Mrs. Epsworth?" echoed the hotel receptionist. "I'm sorry, they checked out this morning."

That took me by surprise. I had the impression the night before that they were planning on staying longer. Why the sudden change of plans? Had Victor gotten the wind up? I explained to the receptionist that I was an old friend of Mrs. Epsworth's and had been hoping to visit her while she was on the Cape. What a shame, the woman said. In fact, she added, the Epsworths *had* originally booked to stay on through Sunday.

"Was Mrs. Epsworth well when she checked out this morning?" I asked, trying to sound solicitous and not just nosey.

"I'm sorry, I really don't know. It was Mr. Epsworth who came to the desk. I didn't see Mrs. Epsworth at all this morning. Mr. Epsworth said she had left earlier."

Tony was waiting for me in the dining room. He had already started his breakfast and paused thoughtfully with a forkful of blueberry pancake raised halfway to his mouth as he listened to my report. He must have shed his skepticism sometime during the night, because he didn't even try to argue with me this time.

"So let's say Freddy Jones knocked Marjorie Epsworth off last night and got rid of her body somehow," he mused. "Maybe he took her out to sea and dumped her in deep water—a regular fishing trip, with no witnesses to anything. And now Victor is carrying on as usual. When do you think he'll report her missing?"

I shook my head in frustration. Why would Victor carry on as usual? Why had he told the woman at the hotel that Marjorie had left earlier? Why hadn't he just reported her missing this morning? *Eccentric millionairess goes walking on beach and disappears*. I could just imagine the headlines. Why would Victor want people to think his wife was still alive?

I picked up my empty coffee cup and looked around for our waitress. There was only one other couple in the dining room; the rest of the diners had all cleared out for the beach or wherever else tourists go on a hot Saturday morning on the Cape. Our waitress was on the other side of the room setting tables and tidying up for the lunch crowd. Her movements were quick and efficient, with not a motion wasted. I caught her eye and held my cup aloft. She nodded and turned toward the kitchen, stopping for a moment to straighten a print on the wall before she disappeared through the swinging doors, presumably on her way to the coffee.

"Well? When do you think he'll report her missing?" Tony repeated.

But I was staring at the print on the far wall of the dining room. It was one of those Cubist representations of modern life that make it impossible for you to tell which side is up. It was a Picasso. "Now wait a minute. . . ."

The waitress came and poured my coffee. She must have thought I was in caffeine shock, because my mouth was hanging open and I must have been glassy-eyed. She shrugged and went back to her work on the other side of the room.

I hit the table with my hand and the coffee sloshed all over the tablecloth. "That's it. The Picasso at the auction. He must plan on buying it. He must be planning on going to the auction after all."

Tony grabbed a napkin and began sopping up the spilled coffee. Then he rose to his feet and pulled my chair out for me. One thing about Tony, when he decides to do something, he does it.

He pointed to his wristwatch. "It's already ten o'clock. If I remember correctly, the auction is supposed to start at eleven. It should take us about that long to get down to Hyannis."

He led the way to the door, tall, lanky, and unmistakably middle-aged in his plaid Bermuda shorts. "I'll get the car. You put in a call to Chief Nutting and tell him what you figured out. Tell him to contact the police in Hyannis and to meet us at the auction. Maybe that'll spur him into action."

●

The man at the door of the Blaring mansion looked disdainfully at Tony's Bermudas and appeared ready to bar the way to us on purely aesthetic grounds until Tony flashed his press card under the man's nose. I've often marvelled at the effect of that small plastic card and never cease to be amazed at how people change their attitude when they see it. The power of the press and all that. The man at the door cleared his throat and switched his greeting from what surely would have been "Sorry, sir. Proper dress is required," to "Of course, sir. Come this way, come this way."

He threw the doors wide open and led us into a circular entrance paved in black and white marble. There he passed us on to a boy with a whispered admonition to make sure we got seats up front, and the boy led us to a large mirrored room that might have once been a ballroom.

About 150 people were in the room, some of them already seated, others milling around in the back making last-minute deals. An auctioneer was standing behind a podium on a small stage at the front of the room.

"Nineteen-hundred-from-the-lady-on-the-right-do-I-hear-two-thousand -who'll-give-me-two-thousand-for-this-chair-in-the-style-of-Louis-the- fifteenth-two-thousand-do-I-hear-two-thousand—*two-thousand*-to-the-gentleman-in-the-front -row-do-I-hear-twenty-one-hundred-twenty-one-hundred. . . ."

I nudged Tony in the ribs. "There he is."

Sure enough, Victor Epsworth was sitting in the second row, in the reserved section, a catalogue in his hand, a leather attaché case on the seat next to him. He was alone. Two seats were vacant directly behind him. The boy cleared the way for us and handed us a catalogue as we slid by the knees of the seated buyers. A woman in a cream silk suit that must have cost almost as much as the phony Louis XV chair just purchased by the gentleman in the front row gave Tony's Bermudas a dirty look and turned pointedly away. I wondered if Tony should try his press card on her.

According to the catalogue, the chair in the style of Louis XV was item number twenty-four. The Picasso drawing, a red and black chalk study of a woman and child, was number fifty-two. Right after the sale of the Picasso there would be an intermission. I stared at the back of Victor Epsworth's neck, wondering how he expected to get away with it. He probably had his wife's half-million right there in the attaché case at his side. He must be planning on bidding for the Picasso, paying for it and . . . then what? Someone would realize Marjorie Epsworth was missing sooner or later. Maybe Victor was planning on running for it right after the auction. Maybe he had a plane waiting for him this very minute at the Hyannis airport. But why buy the Picasso? Why not just take the money and run? What was there about the Picasso that would make him take this risk?

They were bringing out the paintings now. The first was an early Munnings. The auctioneer announced that the bidding would start at twenty thousand.

The woman in the cream suit turned in her chair and motioned to a man sitting behind her. "Have you seen Harvey Littlecomb yet? He said he'd be here early."

The man lowered the opera glasses he was holding to his eyes to get a better view of the horses grazing in the Munnings. He shook his head. "No I haven't. You noticed the Guggenheim and the Museum of Fine Arts have someone here."

"The Guggenheim's after those Klee sketches. The MFA wants the Picasso, but they won't be able to outbid Harvey. They don't have a chance, not with the kind of purse the Metropolitan gave him. He said he's prepared to go as high as seven hundred and fifty thousand, if he has to. I wonder why he's late?"

I remembered last night's conversation, how Marjorie Epsworth had been worried about the man from the Met outbidding her and how her husband had assured her she had nothing to worry about. How did Victor Epsworth know the man from the Met wasn't going to make it this year?

The Munnings went for fifty thousand. "Dirt cheap," the woman in the suit muttered. A watercolor by some American I never heard of went for eighty thousand, and a woman in a big hat covered with flowers paid one hundred thousand for a large oil painting of what looked like a Civil War battlefield.

Next came a series of seascapes. I wouldn't have minded picking up a few of them for our living room back in Concord, but decided to let them go when the bidding started at twelve thousand. I really didn't care for seascapes anyway. Maybe something more classical, more nineteenth-century would come up. Something more *affordable*. There was a bustle in the row in front of us, and I snapped out of my glum contemplation of our modest bank account to see Marjorie Epsworth pushing by the knees and crossed legs of the seated buyers. *Marjorie Epsworth?* What was she doing here? According to all my calculations, she was supposed to be floating with the tide toward George's Bank by now.

She plumped down next to her husband in a froth of lavender taffeta and tulle and crushed her heavy breasts against his arm in an enthusiastic embrace. "Oh Victor, I've just been in the viewing room with the Picasso. It's absolutely marvelous. I just have to have it."

He patted her hand. "There's nothing to worry about. I already told you that. Look, they're bringing it out now."

There was some commotion at the back of the ballroom as the auctioneer started hawking the Picasso at one hundred thousand. I turned my head and caught sight of Chief Nutting. He was pushing through the crowd with a grim-looking man in uniform and I wondered if he had brought in the Mounties. More likely it was someone from the Hyannis police or maybe the state police. Nutting caught my eyes on him and put his index finger to the brim of his cap and lifted it a quarter-inch in what might have been a salute. He was heading in our direction.

I whipped around in my seat, my mind buzzing. Tony was staring straight ahead with a slow flush of red spreading up the back of his neck. I knew he'd never let me forget this. I also knew I had about two minutes to figure out what was going on here before Nutting would call me on the carpet. I could imagine the charges: waking the police chief out of a deep sleep; reaching hasty, illogical and irresponsible conclusions; spreading malicious rumors; wasting the valuable time of public defenders of the peace; forcing public defenders of the peace to attend art auctions.

The bidding on the Picasso got off to a hot start with Marjorie Epsworth shooting up her hand to catch the auctioneer's attention. An elderly man wearing a pince-nez countered her bid with a twitch of his left ear. A heavy-set man in a wrinkled seersucker suit raised his eyebrows and brought the bid to two hundred thousand. Within minutes, the auctioneer had called four hundred thousand and the seersucker suit was shaking his head. It was down to Marjorie and Pince-Nez. Behind the last row of seats, Chief Nutting was craning his neck to catch my attention and I was studiously ignoring him.

"Four-hundred-thousand-I-have-four-hundred-thousand-from-the-gentleman-representing-the-Museum-of-Fine-Arts-do-I-have-four-hundred-twenty-thousand-four-hundred-*four-hundred-twenty*-thousand-from-the-lady-in-lavender—who'll-give-me-four-hundred-forty-thousand-do-I-hear-four-hundred-forty-thousand? Sir? Will you bid four-hundred-forty-thousand-four-hundred-forty-thousand-for-this-fine Picasso-drawing-do-I-hear-four-hundred-forty-thousand? Do-I-hear-four-hundred-thirty-thousand-four-hundred-thirty-thousand? No? Do-I-hear four-hundred-twenty-five-thousand-will-anyone-offer-me-four-hundred-twenty-five-thousand-for-this-early-Picasso-chalk-drawing?"

The man in the pince-nez smoothed his hair down and turned away. It was obvious there were no takers. The auctioneer took a deep breath like a diver poising at the edge of a dock.

"Going-once-for-four-hundred-twenty-thousand-going-twice-do-I-have-any-more-offers-going-goinggg-*sold*-to-the-lady-in-lavender-for-four-hundred-twenty-thousand-dollars."

Marjorie Epsworth squealed in ecstasy and threw her arms around Victor. "Oh Victor, baby. I got it, I got, it, I got it. It's really mine."

Victor Baby extracted himself from her grip and stroked his Van Dyke back into place, looking around with a superior smile at the rest of us. "I told you not to worry. I told you there'd be no problem. Shall we go on up and collect it now?"

I let my breath out in a long sigh. "The man from the Met."

Tony turned to me. His face was still flushed. "What?"

"The man from the Metropolitan Museum—Littlecomb. Why didn't he make it?"

"Maybe he missed the subway. Maybe he took his seven hundred and fifty grand to Sotheby's."

"But if he had been here, the Epsworths never would have gotten the Picasso," I insisted, ignoring the sarcasm in his voice. "You heard Marjorie last night. She said she couldn't go over five hundred thousand."

"Well, he wasn't here. It's a moot point."

"That's right. He wasn't here. Maybe something happened to him so he couldn't make it."

I grabbed Tony's hand and started pushing through the crowd toward Chief Nutting. He had abandoned his post at the back of the seating area and was making his way with the other officer to the front of the room where a crowd had clustered around the auctioned paintings, which were displayed behind velvet ropes. We intercepted him just as he was nearing the Picasso drawing.

"Chief, can I have a word with you?"

Nutting was wearing a clean uniform shirt and had scraped his face clean of whiskers, but he looked as bad-tempered as he had the night before. "Sorry, Mrs. Craighton. I have a job to do."

"But I think you should hear what we have to say. Harvey Little-comb. . . ."

The chief threw his head back and squinted down his nose at me. He signalled the other man to go ahead and lowered his voice. "So you know about that, huh? Some fishermen picked up his body this morning. Freddy Jones admitted everything." He tipped his cap to me. "Guess you heard right after all, Mrs. Craighton, ma'am. Only thing is, you had the wrong victim. Stick around. I'll need you later."

With that, he stepped up to the velvet rope where Marjorie and Victor Epsworth were posing for flashing cameras in front of the Picasso. Victor Epsworth frowned at the intrusion, but that didn't stop Chief Nutting from raising his voice over the excited chatter of the crowd.

"Mr. Epsworth, I have here a warrant for your arrest for conspiracy to murder one Harvey Littlecomb. You have a right to remain silent. . . ."

•

After dinner we went down to the deserted beach and walked to the end of the stone jetty. The tide was coming in and the swirling water made a greedy, gulping sound at the edge of the rocks below our feet. The white eye of the Chatham lighthouse glared at us for a moment, then turned its gaze over the dark liquid expanse where a few boats were still returning to port farther up the channel. Tony put his arm around my shoulders as I began to shiver in the evening breeze.

"Do you think Marjory Epsworth knew her husband was planning to kill Harvey Littlecomb? Could she have wanted the drawing enough to let him murder for it?" I asked.

Tony sighed. "Who knows? If she did, they aren't telling anyone. Whatever the case, Victor must have been so much in love with her that he was willing to go to any length to make sure she got what she wanted. He knew Littlecomb would be able to buy the drawing right out from under her grasp, so he made arrangements to have Littlecomb removed."

It always impressed me how well Tony could put things in neat, logical, understandable order once he had the facts. It was the journalist in him, no doubt. I knew that if I ever tried to explain this to anyone, I'd just make a mess of it.

"Talk about falling for clichés," I groaned. "All I saw was the classic set-up of the younger husband with no money of his own and his rich, spoiled, middle-aged wife with her grip on the purse strings. It seemed so obvious that he was setting up her murder so that he could get his hands on her money."

Tony ruffled my hair. "But you weren't wrong about what you heard. What was it Epsworth said to Freddy Jones? *Make sure there are no witnesses.*' Just think, Chris. If you hadn't heard them talking out here yesterday and reported it to Nutting, no one would ever have been any the wiser. They never would have connected Epsworth to Littlecomb's death."

"His body would have washed up on the beach somewhere and no one would ever have known what happened," I mused. "Nutting would probably have written it off as an accident."

"Well, maybe not. The police aren't *that* dumb."

"Hmmph." I was still smarting from the chief's crack about my getting the victims wrong. Talk about gratitude. I had practically solved the case for him when he didn't even know he *had* a case.

Tony looked sideways at me with that look he gets when he's about to humor me. "At least we got to go to the auction."

I snorted. "It was an educational experience. Twelve thousand dollars for a picture of a sailboat. We could buy a *real* sailboat for that kind of money."

"Not everything was that expensive. Actually, some of the prices were pretty reasonable. You just had to recognize a good buy when you saw it." He dug his hand into his jacket pocket and pulled out a small package wrapped in brown paper and string. "As a matter of fact, I managed to find something I thought you'd like. Just a little momento to remember this vacation by."

I remembered how he had disappeared while I trailed behind Chief Nutting and the Epsworths to the police car in the parking lot of the Blaring estate. Now I realized he must have gone back to the auction. I could see in my mind's eye the pages at the end of the catalogue that pictured some of the jewelry from the estate. The package in my hand was just about the size of a small jewelry case.

I tore the package open. "Tony. You shouldn't have."

The the last sheet of brown paper was lying crumpled on the jetty beside me and I was holding in my hand not a jewelry box but a small wooden carving. It was one of those Tyrolean carvings—folk art at its most kitsch. The figure in the carving was of an old woman leaning with her ear against a door. She was bent over so that her hips jutted out at a ninety-degree angle from the rest of her body. Her face was screwed up in an expression of intense concentration.

Maybe it wasn't a Picasso, and maybe it was just about the last objet d'art I would have chosen from the Blaring collection. But there was one thing I could say about it: I could be sure Tony hadn't resorted to murder to get it for me.

Death on Goose Hill

NITA PENFOLD

*T*he July heat shimmered off the fields of half-grown corn. Black and white Holsteins huddled under whatever shade they could, swatting each other companionably with a swish of their long tails. Only eight o'clock, but already Carlton Corners was bustling, at least as bustling as a farm community could be with only 700 people. I was glad to get into the office. The town council rightly believed a sheriff, even an acting one, couldn't operate efficiently without an air conditioner. I just wished they'd give me another squad car.

Hannah Marks was already at her desk. A rose of a woman, she sat all blooming and plump in her cotton print dress. The ready smile left her face as she saw me. "Emma Mackey, you promised me you were going to stay home this morning and let Alex and Rufus handle things here."

Henry, her brother, looked sideways at me as he put down the morning paper he'd been reading in the waiting area in front of Hannah's desk. "How ya doin', Sheriff?"

"Fine, Henry. A little tired maybe. But this should fix me up." I poured a cup of Hannah's superstrength coffee and picked up a semi-fresh danish from the plate nearby. Hannah still had on her irritated look, like a storm coming. She'd had that same look years before in my tomboy days when she caught me climbing the water tower outside of town—that you-should-be-ashamed-of-yourself look. Then I'd been the sheriff's daughter. Hannah still found it hard to call me sheriff, but she

55

begrudgingly acknowledged my qualifications as acting sheriff, at least until the fall elections when a "proper candidate" could be found. She'd been my father's secretary and our neighbor, coming out of a very short retirement when I was appointed. Probably to keep me in line.

"Well?" Her blue eyes sharpened to ice points.

"Hannah, the federal and state authorities have pretty much taken over. It's fairly routine."

"Posh, that doesn't mean you haven't run yourself ragged all night. Woman, you're gonna wear yourself thin."

Henry ran his hand back and forth through his gray spiky crewcut as if to build up an electric charge. He was wearing old stained workpants, carefully mended and creased by Hannah, with a white T-shirt that kept riding up under the narrow suspenders he perpetually wore. "Not much about the bank robbery in this here paper, Sheriff. Any news yet?"

He must have sensed Hannah's mood and headed her off, much like he used to do when I was a kid. I could have hugged him. "Only things we know for sure are that the suspect wore a stocking mask, brandished a handgun, and used one of the employees as a shield to force his way into the bank before it opened. He's medium-built and right-handed."

"That's not much to go on, Sheriff. That description could fit half the men in the county, including me." Henry chuckled a little, pleased at counting himself as a suspect. "Maybe even some of the women." He eyed Hannah.

"Whoever it was herded all the bank employees into the vault and escaped with two sacks of small bills. At last tally, almost one hundred grand. The suspect took off in an old light green Chevy Nova. We got a partial plate number from a witness over in Burdock Crossing who almost got run over. Most of that information will be in the paper tomorrow."

Hannah interrupted. "First thing this morning, the state authorities called and Alex went over. Seems the Nova was reported stolen night before last from somewhere over the Erie County line."

"Then whoever robbed the bank has probably ditched the car by now." I gratefully gulped down some of the steaming coffee and felt it burn into my stomach, hoping the caffeine would kick in soon. "Ah, just what I needed."

The phone rang before Hannah could give me her have-a-good-break-fast speech. "Sheriff's office. Yes, she's here. Calm down, Charlene. Hold on a minute." She pushed the hold button.

"Charlene Walters up on Goose Hill?" Henry asked.

I put down the coffee. "What's the problem?"

"She says somebody tried to shoot her!" Hannah's emphasis was definitely on the *says*.

"Don't you believe her?"

"Emma, she's got to be one of the most mean-spirited women I've ever met. Some kids were probably target-shooting and she wants to get them in trouble."

Henry tightened the clip on his left suspender. "More likely one of the customers she's been accused of cheating at that roadside stand of hers. Barney says she weights the scales. The council's been thinking about suspending her sales permit."

"Tell her I'll come up."

Hannah relayed the message, but as she hung up, the phone buzzed again. "Sheriff's office. Yes, Ed, what's up? Okay." She put the phone down. "Edwin Freihoffer. He says there's been a shooting up on Goose Hill, and to get right over there."

"Did he say who got shot?"

"No, Emma, just that there'd been a shooting."

"I'm on my way." I made sure my .38 special was loaded and then strapped it tightly into its holster at my side.

Henry stood up hopefully. "Need any help?"

"Henry, I need you to stay here until Rufus shows up. Pete picked a bad week to go fishing."

Henry nodded. Pete Syczinski was my number-one deputy. Alex at least had some police training, but Rufus was a trainee, if there was such a thing in this town. The extent of his police knowledge consisted of what he had picked up in a $600 mail-order police enforcement correspondence course. I suspected that he hadn't even completed that. He was a freckle-faced eighteen-year-old who looked out of place in our tan uniforms, although he'd probably say the same for me.

"Hannah, get Alex over as soon as you can, and send the emergency squad."

She waved me out the door.

Alex had our one cruiser, so I got into my Jeep and rammed the portable light against the dashboard, flipping on my tinny siren. A few townspeople turned my way as I headed out to the west of town. The cows ignored me.

Goose Hill rose to one of the higher elevations in the township. There were two ways of getting there. The long way was about seven miles over paved roads. The short way took four miles off the journey but the road appeared to be a goose track up the side of a cliff, hence its name. Every time it rained, a few more chunks of the dirt track eroded, and the town wouldn't vote to have it paved considering the angle of descent. Each year, at least one kid would venture down on a dare or a joyride on his or her bike and end up breaking some bone or another. No one lived at the summit anymore. There was the old Miller homestead, which had been condemned; the rest of the area contained small produce farms and a few dairy herds farther down on the far side of the hill.

When I'd gotten this job, I'd made a point of going door-to-door throughout the whole township, talking with the residents, telling them about what I hoped to accomplish. Some of them appreciated it; others (like Charlene Walters) seemed extremely uncomfortable having the new sheriff at their front doors. Whether because I was a woman, or because they were doing something illegal, I couldn't tell. Hannah told me later that a lot of the old-timers didn't think it was appropriate. They thought the crime rate would skyrocket if everyone knew there was a woman sheriff. But then Henry twinkled and added that their wives sure did find it interesting to have a woman in charge.

The Freihoffer place stood near a stand of pines on Willow Road down from the junction with Goose Hill Road. I knew that Ed had retired there with his wife, Ambrosia, after they'd stopped working at the toy factory over in the next county. The small, solid clapboard house with wide front porch perched next to a garage and a green-shingled shed. Their produce stand sat empty out by the driveway but I could see the trimmed lawn spreading down to at least an acre of vegetables planted in neat green rows bordering the woods. The smell of freshly-mown grass was hanging on the heated air.

Ed was leaning over something on the ground when he heard my siren and stood up to meet me. He was taller than my own five feet, seven inches and a lean man, except for a pot belly pushing his green T-shirt and workpants out as if he had swallowed a small sack of flour. There were tears in his bloodshot blue eyes, and he wiped more of them out of the craggy lines on his face with a frayed red bandanna.

"You gotta arrest her, Sheriff Mackey. She had no call to shoot them, no call at all."

Them? "Now, Mr. Freihoffer, exactly who got shot?"

He pointed to the ground. "My cats, 'Brosia shot my cats. I want her arrested."

I followed him over to where six mangy skin-and-bones cats lay stretched out on the lawn. They'd all been shot, pretty cleanly too. Flies buzzed the corpses. There were two calicos, a blackie, and the rest were a mottled assortment of brown, black, and tan.

Life in the country; I didn't know whether to laugh or to cry. First a bank robbery, then cat homicide, or was it feline-acide? I tried to keep a straight face as I turned back to Edwin and got him to tell me what had happened. He sat down tiredly on the front porch steps and told me how he had come back from his weekly visit to his sister's to find the cats dead, neatly laid out on the lawn.

"'Brosia's been nagging at me about them for weeks. This morning, 'fore I left, she said that iffin I didn't get rid of them, she would." He looked up. "I never thought she'd murder them, Sheriff. Or I never woulda left."

"Mr. Freihoffer, I realize that you're upset, but do you really want to pursue charges?"

"Yeah, I want her charged with cat murder—first degree. It'll show her she can't go around shooting pets just 'cause she don't like them."

"The most the charge could be is destruction of private property. How long have you owned the cats, and can you prove it?"

"Well," he looked doubtful, "I've had them about five weeks or so. They's strays mostly, so I don't have no papers or anything."

"Where's your wife?"

"She's in the house."

I pulled open the front screen door and stepped into the cool house. There was a long flowered sofa along one pine wall, and an oval braided rug with bright shades of blue and green on the polished floor. Ambrosia Freihoffer sat on an old stuffed rocking chair, a rifle propped across the arms. Her feet were up on a mismatched hassock.

For one insane moment, I thought maybe she was planning on using that gun again. I've found that people can go just as crazy in the country as they do in the city, for about the same basic reasons: loneliness, depression, being driven to the end of their endurance and seeing no way out. Then I spotted the cleaning kit on her broad lap and the oily rag in her hand. I relaxed.

Ambrosia was as big as her husband but wider, with a large bosom that pushed against her sleeveless print blouse like an underlying log. She had wild gray curls that she'd failed to capture with black bobby pins. Her long skinny legs stuck up out of loose brown shorts. Getting closer, I noticed her legs were spotted with raised hives or bites, and around her ankles they had swollen so that her canvas shoes barely fit.

"Hello, Sheriff." Ambrosia was practically shouting and beamed at me as if she were pleased that I'd come calling. "Would you like some lemonade?" She set the cleaning kit and the rifle down on the floor.

"No, thank you, ma'am." It was hard to know where to begin in the face of her cheerfulness.

She looked puzzled, then laughed. "Just a minute. I gotta get my hearing aid back in. Took it out when I was shootin'." She took a small plastic device from her pocket and fit it into her ear.

"Edwin tells me that you shot his cats."

She nodded, brown eyes large behind the big-framed glasses she wore. "Why?"

Ambrosia shifted in the rocker. "'Cause of them damn fleas. Pardon my language, Sheriff."

I fought down a smile. "Certainly."

"He started feedin' a couple of strays last month sometime and then they musta got the word out 'cause there was a half-dozen after awhile. Now, most days I don't mind cats. He kept them outside and all, but the fleas would jump onto Edwin and he'd just carry them on into the house. They don't bother him none, just me. Look at my legs. It got so's I was dreamin' 'bout fleas jumpin' on me and I couldn't sleep no more. I had the gardenin' and sewin' and cannin' to do. He wouldn't do nothing 'bout them, so's I just had to get rid of them. What else could I do?"

I was saved from answering that flea collars might have been an alternative when the phone rang. It was Hannah letting me know that

Charlene had called three more times and Alex had gone over to placate her, but she still insisted on seeing me. I told Hannah to cancel the paramedics. I excused myself as best I could from the Freihoffers with a promise to return.

Charlene Walters was actually the Freihoffer's next-door neighbor, as country neighbors go. About a hundred yards down Willow Road, the pavement curved and there rested a rickety board stand with "Walters Produce" stenciled crudely on the side. It looked like the paint was the only thing holding it together. A few baskets of brownish peas and an old hanging scale were balanced on the board that ran across the front.

Charlene's ranch house seemed sturdier than her stand, but the white paint was peeling badly. I remembered Martha Rebinsky telling me she'd never work for her again after she stiffed her on weeding and hauling trash—Charlene positive that she'd said twenty instead of forty for the job. Martha's a good kid, working to pay her way through agricultural college at Alfred. Charlene wanted her to paint the house too, but Martha had held out for the money up front. Martha said that Charlene had puffed up like an indignant rooster and wondered what had happened to young people these days that they didn't trust the word of their elders. Obviously, she hadn't found anyone else to paint.

Charlene met me on the enclosed side porch in tight pink jogging shorts and a matching shirt. She was at least ten years younger than the Freihoffers; for the most part thin, with muscular legs. The skin on her upper arms hung loose in folds as if she had once weighed much more. I felt like an awkward giant beside her and could see patches of her scalp right through her short-clipped hennaed hair. Charlene looked rather like a kewpie doll gone punk with garish red lipstick, heavy rouge, and purple eyeshadow slathered above cloudy-blue eyes. She gave me a surprisingly strong handshake for her size, with a hand covered in Band-Aids.

"Got into a thornbush," she mumbled, withdrawing her hand carefully. "Nice of you to come all the way up here." There was an edge of sarcasm to her high voice. "Your deputy and I were just going over the facts."

Alex had never looked so relieved to see me. He was used to handling drunks down at the Mighty Eagle, or stopping folks for speeding through the main part of town. "Hello, Sheriff. Mrs. Walters here was just telling me how Mrs. Freihoffer has been out to get her since she opened up her produce stand." He rose to his full six feet from a wicker chair that looked ready to collapse into its twin.

"Ambrosia has been downright *niggardly*, if you know what I mean." She emphasized the word and watched Alex's face carefully.

His brown eyes widened, but with effort, he ignored the racial slur. I didn't. "Now, Mrs. Walters, there is no call to. . . ."

"Oh, I meant no offense by that, Deputy," Charlene said in a cloying tone. "I just meant that she's very stingy. She wasn't pleased when I opened my vegetable stand. Didn't want the competition. And then both her and Edwin objected last month when I cut a footpath through the woods so that I could run in the mornings. My doctor said I needed the exercise. They never even use those woods. No, they've just been out for blood since I inherited this place from my husband's family two years ago."

I asked Charlene to go over the morning's events. She said that she'd taken her run as usual that morning, about six-thirty, before it got hot. She started at her house, ran through the woods which cut through the Freihoffer's property to Goose Hill Road, and then around the corner to Willow Road and home. It was a rough elongated triangle that took her anywhere from a half-hour to forty-five minutes depending on her stamina. She'd been interrupted that morning by gunfire.

"I declare, I was so scared when that bullet went whizzing past me and hit. . . ." Charlene suddenly stopped, a rather sly look on her face, like a cat waiting to pounce on a mouse. "A tree, that's it, it must have hit a tree. Anyway, I just came right back here and called your office."

"How do you know that it was Mrs. Freihoffer?" Alex asked.

'Well, I saw her, of course, standing on her lawn waving that rifle around. I thought my days on this earth were numbered. She's a dangerous woman, Sheriff. She should be locked up. You mark my words, one of these days, she'll kill someone." Charlene said this last with utter certainty.

"For your information, Mrs. Walters, Mrs. Freihoffer was killing some stray cats, not aiming at you."

"Is that what she told you, Sheriff? Well, I'm not surprised. She knew that she missed me and needed an alibi. I want to press charges, attempted murder."

This was a morning for people who wanted to press charges. "Well, we'll have to do some further investigating. Why don't you show Deputy Conners here exactly where you were shot at, while I go talk to the Freihoffers." This was turning out to be one hell of a morning. Sometimes I felt this job required degrees in psychology and sociology more than one in law enforcement. I almost wished that I'd kept my promise to Hannah and slept late.

Edwin was still on his front porch. "Do you want these here bodies for evidence, Sheriff, or can I bury them?"

"Things have gotten a bit more complicated, Mr. Freihoffer." I explained about Charlene's accusations.

The color rose in his face. "That woman's a damn liar! 'Brosia would never shoot anywheres near a person. Even somebody as mean as Charlene." He called his wife out onto the porch. She was drying her hands on her apron. "'Brosia, that Walters woman says you tried to shoot her!"

Ambrosia Freihoffer's face went from bewilderment to comprehension to anger. "That biddy. She can't do that, can she, Sheriff?"

"'Course not," Edwin intoned. For a man who had been going to charge his wife with cat murder, he was suddenly solicitous of her rights. He was hard to figure.

"Why don't we just go over it slowly?" I said. "Did you see Charlene at all?"

"Why, yes, I saw her running to beat the devil in that purple suit of hers when I was up on the side lawn toward the front. Never thought she could move that fast."

"What time was that?"

"Oh, well after seven-thirty, I should think."

"And you didn't shoot at any of the cats up there?"

"No, they was all dead by then and I'd laid them out for Edwin to bury when he got back."

I had Ambrosia show me exactly where she'd killed the cats. Edwin walked along with her. There were six places with blood present. All were away from the road. She couldn't remember the order but she was sure that the last one died pretty far into the woods toward Goose Hill Road because it had taken her several shots to hit it. I could see an abandoned truck rusting out between the pines, a dilapidated plow hanging from its front like a loose tooth.

"Miller used to drag his trash over there and leave it." Edwin had a hand on his wife's shoulder as we walked back toward the house, the grasshoppers springing around us in the garden as we picked our way through the rows. "Sheriff, what's gonna happen now?"

"There'll probably be a hearing, but unless there's more evidence or an eyewitness, it will be Charlene's word against Ambrosia's, and the charges will most likely be dropped. But you should get a lawyer." I paused. "What about your charges?"

"I plumb forgot about them." He looked at his wife with a kind of fierceness at first, then with resignation mixed with affection. "I guess I should've listened to you better. I didn't think things was gettin' that bad."

Ambrosia hugged her husband. "I'm sorry, too, Edwin. Maybe we could get some other critter around here for you. One that don't get fleas."

A siren broke through the morning's oppressiveness. I figured Hannah hadn't had time to cancel the paramedics, then the truck flashed by the turnoff to Willow Road and continued down Goose Hill, followed by Rufus's Mustang. I could hear the phone ringing at Freihoffers', and Edwin sprinted up to the back door.

"For you, Sheriff," he called.

It was Hannah again. "Things always come in threes, Emma. Report of a car accident on Goose Hill; the Rogers boy called it in. I sent Rufus with strict instructions not to touch anything. Henry went with him."

I could see Alex down on the corner of the property with Charlene and yelled to him to meet me when he was finished. He waved okay. I told the Freihoffers I'd get back to them later and got the jeep moving around the corner to Goose Hill Road.

Rufus was already roping off the area and the paramedics were putting their equipment away as I arrived. Hal Winston shoved his thick glasses back up his nose as he saw me. "He's a goner, Sheriff. We left him just the way we found 'im."

"Call Doc Meyers on your radio and ask her to bring Millie Campbell up with her."

Hal nodded and went back with his partner to wait for the coroner.

A light blue Datsun pick-up rested against a good-sized oak on the right side of the road facing toward Willow Road, so the driver must have crossed over to the wrong side. The front end was crushed in, so he'd obviously been traveling at a fair clip. Something bothered me about that, but I didn't take the time to put my finger on it—just filed the feeling away for later.

The passenger door was open. A man's body lay across the front seat with his hand stretched out as if he had pushed the door open, or was grabbing for it. He was wearing jeans and a faded blue T-shirt. His head was a bloody mass of hair and flesh. I tried to keep a professional, impersonal view, but my stomach was remembering the danish I had wolfed down and wanted very much to get rid of. I swallowed hard. This was one part of the job I couldn't get used to.

There were little plugs of safety glass on the cab's floor and under the dead man's arms. They seemed to have come from the side window. The windshield was cracked where the driver must have hit it. His seat belt wasn't fastened. I shook my head. What a waste.

I carefully popped open the glove compartment and pulled the registration. One Wallace Hopkins over in Strykersville owned the truck. Unless, of course, this was Wallace Hopkins. I didn't want to disturb the body but I could see a wallet sticking out of his back pocket where the body was twisted across the seat. I eased it out. William Hopkins, same address, age twenty-three.

Rufus appeared at my arm. "I cordoned off the area, Sheriff. The Rogers boy is over by that stump if you want to talk to him now." He paused. "Horrible, ain't it?"

I looked into his clear-eyed innocence. The dead man wasn't much older than he was. "Yeah, pretty bad. You did a good job, Rufus."

"Thanks." He blushed and turned away.

Willie Rogers was about eleven, lean and wiry and brown from working the fields with his father. He was fairly leaping with excitement. "He's dead, ain't he? I thought so when he didn't move at all."

I nodded. "Tell me exactly how you found him, Willie."

"Well, I was in the barn doing my chores, hoping I'd be done in time to go to town with my dad. He's out in the back field fixing a torn fence. Anyways, I heard this big crash. But I didn't want to leave the barn—my dad'd skin me alive if I didn't get my chores done. So I finished up first, then came down here to look. When I saw the guy bleeding like that, I ran back up and called." He rattled it off so fast I could barely understand him.

"Where's your mom?"

"She's visiting her cousin, Maude. She just had a baby. Maude, not my mom."

"What time do you think it was when you heard the crash?"

"I don't know. Way after breakfast. That was at six-thirty, right after milking."

"How long had you been working in the barn?"

"An hour or more, I couldn't tell for sure."

"When you found the truck, did you touch anything, or open the door?"

"Oh, no, ma'am. It was already open when I got there."

"Okay, Willie. Thanks for your help. You get back home and tell your dad what's happened."

"Yeah, wait 'til I tell the guys, they'll never believe it." He ran off down the road.

Henry was out pacing off the tire tracks. I like to think of him as my special consultant. He seems to know an awful lot about everything.

"Anything unusual, Henry?"

"Well, Sheriff, see the way these tracks swerve off here? Looks like he was trying to avoid hitting something."

"Or maybe something startled him and he lost control?"

"Could be."

I looked down the road to the Miller place, then across into the woods. I could see that old rusted truck through the brush. The thought that had been bothering me before came back full force. "Henry, where was this guy coming from in such a hurry? He couldn't have come up the ravine end of Goose Hill, even in that truck." I called to Rufus that I was going to look around and to watch for the coroner. He nodded and sat down on a stump.

I walked down the road, followed by Henry. The Miller place had a big condemned sign on it, but the side door was still functional, and it stood wide open. A sleeping bag and some canned goods sat on the floor in the back room. So this guy had been camping out here. Not long enough to get comfortable, though.

We went back outside. There was a shack in decent condition behind the house, with tire tracks pushing down the high grass leading up to it. I opened the worn double doors. An old Chevy Nova, light green, sat inside. I checked the plate number then took a handkerchief out, covered the door handle, and opened it. On the floor was a piece of pantyhose and a canvas bag with "Wyoming County Savings Bank" stenciled on the side.

Henry ran his hand through his hair. "Looks like you got yourself a bank robber, Sheriff."

"Yes, a dead one."

Henry and I started back to the accident site. The morning's events went round and round in my head like a carnival ride gone berserk. What were the odds against all these incidents coinciding on the same morning without being connected somehow? Accused on several occasions of having an overly tidy mind, I tend to relish cause and effect rather than randomness and feel strongly that there are patterns in everything if you look hard enough. It is comforting to me, I suppose, to think that I will get an answer when I ask, Why?

So what did I have? A woman shooting her husband's cats, a woman accusing her neighbor of trying to kill her, and a bank robber dead in a car accident. Not a usual morning's work. I stopped walking. We were about even with where the tire tracks swerved.

I had the beginnings of an idea. "Henry, say you were this young bank robber, maybe your first heist, and you're holed up in the Miller place when you are startled by gunfire. What would you do?

Henry rubbed his chin. "I see what you're gettin' at, Sheriff. If I were a tetch on the nervous side, I might just panic, grab the money, and get the hell outta there."

"Right. So you're tooling down the road and suddenly your side window breaks in."

"Hold on a minute. Why do you say that? It coulda happened in the crash."

"That guy was lying on top of the safety glass, so it must have broken before he crashed."

"Okay. I admit he was probably going pretty fast, and that might've been enough to make him lose control." Henry looked confused. "But what broke the window?"

"Come on." I explained to Henry about the dead cats as I pulled him down the rough-cut path into the woods. The old truck sat up on concrete blocks about twenty feet in. It didn't take us long to find the ricochet mark on the front of the plow; probably just the right angle to send one of Ambrosia's bullets skirting toward Goose Hill Road.

Henry looked at me with admiration. "You sure are smart, Sheriff."

"Thanks, but it's really just being stubborn about finding answers."

"But wait a minute. Wouldn't Ambrosia have heard the crash and called it in?"

"She told me she'd taken her hearing aid out while she was shooting, so I don't think she would have."

By the time we returned to the accident site, everyone had arrived. Millie Campbell, a skinny woman in safari shorts who worked for the local paper and doubled as our police photographer, was snapping pictures of the tire tracks and the truck. Cynthia Meyers, the coroner, had her squat body wedged into the cab of the truck, examining the dead man. Alex and Rufus were leaning up against the cruiser, and the paramedics had already left.

I told Alex to get hold of the state and federal people. Cynthia motioned me over to the truck.

"I can't do much more here. I can tell you, though, that this man did not die from the accident unles that tree got up and hit him over the head."

"What do you mean?"

"Those head injuries are inconsistent with hitting the windshield. Plus he's got what look like wood splinters in his scalp. My educated guess is that someone clobbered him with a hunk of wood after the crash. No shortage of that around here. But I'll have to autopsy to be sure."

"Can you give me a time of death?"

"Now, Emma, I know you have to ask, but I just can't be that accurate, especially in this heat." She wiped a tissue across her forehead and under her chin. "Off the record, I'd say not more than two or three hours ago, tops. Do you want me to take the body when Millie is through?"

I explained about the possible connection with the bank robbery and Cynthia nodded her gray-streaked head. "Those good ol' boys will want to do their own investigation. Well, let them. I'm not looking for extra work. Take care, Sheriff. Hope you won't need me again soon."

I asked Millie to get as many shots of the body and surrounding area as she could before the troopers arrived. Henry followed after her, asking all sorts of technical questions about her equipment. Alex reported that there was an accident up on the highway so the troopers couldn't spare any men for at least forty-five minutes to an hour.

I looked at my watch. A little past nine-thirty in the morning, and I had a dead man, a murderer on the loose, and a uniform that was sticking uncomfortably to my sweaty body. Not a great morning. My wish was that this guy had a partner who stiffed him for the bank money. But my instincts told me that everything was still connected. There was no solid evidence of a second person back at the Miller place, nor in the car. And no money or gun. Whoever killed him must have gotten both. So, even though I disliked the idea, the murderer was most likely someone in the immediate area. I mentally crossed off the Rogers boy from my list. He was too excited just to find the guy. That left the Freihoffers, Charlene Walters, or one of the other farmers down the road.

I explained the situation to Alex and Rufus. I was banking on this being a spur-of-the-moment crime. The murderer probably grabbed the nearest object to strike with, and then either dropped or threw it into the woods. Cynthia had been right about there being no shortage of wood—someone had obviously been adding to their woodpile and left chunks scattered around near the front of where the truck stood. Rufus jumped up and started searching. I stopped Alex from following him.

"Where was it that Charlene said Ambrosia shot at her?"

Alex looked through his notepad. "Right over where their properties meet." He flipped his notes back into his shirt pocket. "Remember when she was babbling about the bullet hitting a tree? Well, the place she showed me had no trees and I couldn't find anything else it could have hit."

"Maybe she was exaggerating."

"I'd say so. That woman gives me the creeps, always looking at you out of the corner of her eyes like that." He shrugged and joined Rufus in the search.

Well, I thought to myself, what if she weren't exaggerating? I already had one connection with Ambrosia and the accident. Wouldn't it be logical to assume another? What if Ambrosia thought that Charlene had seen something she shouldn't have? A woman capable of shooting six cats in cold blood might just be capable of murder. Especially with all that money involved. She was certainly strong enough to have hit the guy over the head. If she were coming back through the woods and saw Charlene on her run, maybe she decided to get rid of any witnesses. And then cleverly set me up about the hearing aid.

I shook my head. I was beginning to see deceit everywhere. The timing didn't seem right somehow. Charlene would have been finished with her run by then, according to her story. And why had she waited so long to complain to my office? It must have been almost an hour later that we got her call. Of course, Charlene seemed one for appearances and probably took the time to change and make herself up after running. Unless Ambrosia was mistaken about the purple suit she said Charlene was wearing, and maybe about the time she saw her. My head was spinning again. Someone was definitely lying. Both stories would have to be checked again.

A sudden shout from Rufus brought us all running. A few yards from the truck, Rufus had found a chopped wedge about a foot long and five or six inches wide. The whole piece was splintered. A brown sticky substance coated one end. I had Millie photograph it before I allowed Rufus to pick it up, using a thin plastic sheet from the scene-of-the-crime kit.

"Shit!" He dropped it to the ground.

"What's wrong?"

Alex looked at Rufus's hand and laughed. "Only splinters, Sheriff. Went right through the plastic. He'll live."

About five things clicked in my head like beads being dropped together onto a string. I told Rufus to wait there with Millie and Henry for the troopers. Alex and I stored the evidence in the cruiser, and I told him what I had in mind, sending him the long way around, while I took the path through the woods.

She was in the corner of her backyard wearing a loose smock with large pockets, trying to get a fire started with some newspapers in an old metal barrel.

"Well, welcome back, Sheriff. Have you arrested Ambrosia yet?" She came toward me.

"No, Mrs. Walters. There have been some other developments—a death on Goose Hill."

"An accident, how awful!" Her elaborately penciled eyebrows shot up.

"I didn't say it was an accident." I could see Alex coming around from the far side of Charlene's weedy vegetable patch. I motioned him over to the barrel.

Charlene was between us and glanced from Alex to me and back again.

"Didn't you know that you have to have a permit for open burning?" I nodded to Alex.

He kicked the barrel, dumping its contents onto the lawn.

"How dare you make such a mess on my property!" She tried to push Alex away from the smoldering rubbish. He grabbed her arms and held her. I stomped out the traces of fire and pulled a purple running suit out of the trash. It was only slightly singed and had dark brown splotches on it. Under it was a black canvas bag.

Charlene was sputtering and struggling to get out of Alex's grip. "How dare you!"

"Now, Mrs. Walters, we are just trying to uphold the law." Alex tried to soothe her.

I wasn't as pleasant. "Can you tell me how you got so much blood on your running suit? And what about those splinters on your hands? That's the real reason you're wearing Band-Aids, isn't it?"

She suddenly stopped struggling and looked me straight in the eye. "What blood, Sheriff? Just some preserves I spilled. And I told you, I got into a thornbush."

I decided to lay everything on the line. "Well, Charlene, I've got a dead man. And a witness who can place you running from the scene. I've got what the lab will confirm is the man's blood on the clothing you were seen wearing this morning. And probably your fingerprints on the door of the truck."

The fire seemed to drain out of her, and Alex let go of her arms. I read her the Miranda rights and she waived them wearily.

"You didn't lie, did you—that bullet went whizzing past you. Right there on the path to Goose Hill. Why don't you tell me what happened?"

Charlene nodded. "I saw the accident. I was going to help, I was. Then I saw the money. All that lovely money."

Charlene's head hung down; she had the defeated look of an abused dog I'd once seen. "You don't know what it's been like, scrimping and saving since my husband died." Her voice became bitter. "He'd borrowed against his life insurance and I was left with nothing but this stupid house from his dead aunt."

"Why didn't you ask for some help? The town's got a fund to help people out."

"I wasn't about to ask my neighbors for charity; I can stand on my own feet, thank you very much, Mrs. Nosey Sheriff."

I returned to the subject of the crime. "So you went through the woods after Ambrosia saw you in order to bring the money back, didn't you?"

She slid her hands into the pockets of her smock, the defiant look returning to her face. "It was self-defense, you know. That man came to and grabbed at me; he had hold of my sleeve. I had to hit him to make him let go."

The gun came up so fast out of her smock pocket that I barely believed it. I was on the ground and rolling, my .38 out as Charlene fired the first shot. Alex lunged for her hand but she got a second round off that caught him in the arm, and he went down.

I couldn't get a clear shot without the chance of hitting Alex, so I held my fire as Charlene took off running down the path.

Alex waved me on. "I'll be okay."

I sprinted after Charlene, firing a shot into the air. But she didn't slow. I could see her a few yards ahead of me, her smock flying back from her is if there were a stiff wind blowing.

As she broke into the open on Goose Hill Road, I had narrowed the space between us to only a few feet. She turned toward me, her face red with exertion and shiny with sweat. I was coming too fast to stop as she fired, so I darted in and out of the trees for cover. She fired again, wildly, then headed toward the crest of Goose Hill beyond the Miller place. We were both out in the open now. I yelled at her to stop and fired again into the air. She couldn't have many bullets left. I expected her to turn at the top of the drop-off.

To this day, I don't know if Charlene knew that she had no hope of getting away or if she just didn't care to try any more. But she ran full tilt over the ridge, screaming as she went, with her smock flapping behind her like a pair of wings.

When the state troopers entered her house later that afternoon, we discovered a few sticks of rickety furniture, a few withered vegetables, and some canned soup. Tubes of makeup that Charlene had used to keep up appearances lay on a scarred old table. We found the money hidden in some rusty coffee cans in the basement, and as far as the troopers were concerned, the case was closed.

Carlton Corners settled back into its daily routine. I see Ambrosia and Edwin in town at least once a week when they come for supplies. They proudly walk their new scampering pure-bred beagle pup—the one with the prominent orange flea collar.

The Whisper Business

DEBORAH HANSON

*A*melia wished she were wearing anything but black. Perhaps scarlet, though even ivory would be better. If she had known how the day would develop, she could have dressed with slightly less dignity for her luncheon at Bullock's Wilshire, where elderly women, such as herself, fragile as porcelain teacups, took their afternoon meal with conversation.

"There must be precious little worth whispering about these days if you are reduced to dredging up a story from this dry well," Claire Foster had said at lunch, carefully replacing a strand of hair gone astray from her upsweep, a graceful gesture from the days before Technicolor. Claire had played cool Hitchcock-type blondes, and she still had an arctic elegance, now iced in platinum. "I haven't made a picture in twenty-six years. What will we talk about?"

They had talked about the past. Then Amelia returned to the newspaper to file her Sunday feature and had heard about Broady. Her black wool crepe suit was appropriate for a murder scene, she supposed, but it seemed to absorb the grime right out of the oily, stagnant air of the warehouse where Broady had his office. Worse, it looked like mourning when just the opposite was true.

"Where is he?" she asked at the door where the coroner's assistants waited with their stretcher, arms folded, used to the delays of homicide. A plainclothes cop stepped aside to show her the body of Mr. Jerry Broady.

"I'm looking for Detective Spiegal."

"That's me," a young man said, surfacing from behind the desk where Broady's body sprawled. "Can I help you?"

She showed him her press card. "I'm Amelia Crater with the *Times*."

"The gossip columnist. Don't tell me this old guy was a somebody?"

"I once knew him," Amelia said.

"Look, I'm sorry," he said.

She scarcely heard him, so intent was her concentration on the corpse. She had to exert an enormous amount of self-restraint to keep herself from picking up Broady's head by a fistful of hair to make damn sure he had breathed his last. She could not quite decide whether it was propriety or revulsion that stopped her.

"You're here by yourself?" Spiegal asked. "This is a pretty rough neighborhood. Make sure an officer walks you back to your car." She knew he wondered why the paper had not sent someone younger to cover the crime. On an everyday killing such as this, a cub reporter usually wrote the story from the police blotter at L.A.P.D. headquarters. Detective Spiegal had no way of knowing that Broady's murder was anything but run-of-the-mill. When one of the most hated men in Hollywood turns up dead, there is a good possibility a scoop can be had, and a scoop was just what Amelia wanted. After forty years of snacking on celebrity tidbits, she had worked up a big appetite for hard news. And if ever a story was hers, it was this one. She had been gathering background information her entire professional life.

"What happened to him?" Amelia asked.

"Looks like robbery-murder. Same old, same old, I'm afraid. Dead from a bullet wound to the chest. The killer must have panicked when he found Broady here, shot and ran. There isn't much, if anything, missing. Mr. Broady's wallet was still in his pocket," Spiegal said. "A sad business." Sad for her to see an old crony leaking all over the floor, an easy victim of a senseless crime, is what the detective meant.

"Murdered," Amelia said. "Not heart failure?" There was surprisingly little gore, but then, he had always been a bloodless son-of-a-bitch.

"No. Nothing natural. Hard to figure why anybody would pick this old guy, but junkies in this neighborhood will end you for a dime."

"Junkies?" Amelia thought that a junkie would not be too panicked to pick the man's pocket for cash. Wouldn't the greater risk be missing the next fix? All Spiegal could see in Broady was a harmless old coot, but then he lacked the benefit of back-story to which Amelia was privy.

"That's my theory, anyway," Spiegal said.

"Oh, I see," Amelia said. Twenty years ago she could have handed Spiegal the Los Angeles telephone book and told him to start looking for murder suspects under A, but most of Broady's old enemies were dead now, or past caring. Had some demented fool finally done the dirty work that so many had privately planned? Or was this busy detective seeking an expedient solution? Unless someone gave him reason to believe otherwise, Amelia felt sure he would file this one under unsolved street crime and not lose any sleep. Amelia was not convinced of his theory, but she wanted a look around before she voiced opinions to the contrary.

"Looks like this Mr. Broady had fallen on hard times," Spiegal said, sounding embarrassed for someone. Broady? Or Amelia? Or just the indecencies of old age? He fidgeted, as though he were looking for any way out of Broady's gone-to-rot office, the floor stacked high with mimeographed pamphlets promising "You Are On Your Way to Hollywood Stardom!"

Indeed, Broady had fallen. Amelia had no idea how far or how hard until now. True, she had not seen him slithering around town in years, but she assumed he would turn a profit even on the wrong side of a rock, and here he had been, peddling his empty dreams to people who could not afford the luxury of real ones. The police moved around the office like archaeologists excavating an ancient tomb, sifting through the dusty scrap heap of earthly remains, careful not to disturb the dead.

"He used to be one of the most powerful men in Hollywood, if you can believe it. Public relations for actors. He managed their careers," she said. Nineteen forty-three, or forty-four. He might have dropped off a turnip truck he looked like such a rube in his too-big blue serge suit, oozing into Los Angeles, a big toothy grin smeared across his face, always a "Howareyadoin, my dear . . . my boy," on his slick lips. The more he tried to ingratiate himself, the more of a laughingstock he became. Amelia had looked into his eyes, glassy black marbles that never knew what expression his mouth was pretending and recognized the rube for what he was, a man who was desperate to have the last laugh. And back then publicity men like Broady and newspaper columnists like Amelia made a difference, everybody had so much to hide.

The coroner's assistants started to scrape Broady's remains off the desk. Amelia no longer questioned his death and turned away. He had been gruesome enough in life. Spiegal turned on the answering machine. A woman's voice with a British accent said: "You have reached Broady Entertainment Enterprises. All lines are busy. For your convenience, your call has been electronically switched to an automatic answering service. Please leave your message at the tone."

"Mr. Jerry Broady was always a stickler for appearances," Amelia said. In reality, he had never achieved more than a shabby imitation of real success. She sighed and lit a cigarette as they loaded the starring attraction onto the gurney and carted him out of the office. On the floor lay a gilt-framed photograph, the glass shattered. Who was this sweet armpiece? Amelia wondered, picking it up. So many starlets had passed through Broady's Rolodex, she could not begin to name them all. This one looked tender and sad despite her 'sixties sex-kitten pout. It was the kind of photograph the *Times* would run next to one of a sheet-draped corpse beneath the headlines. "Holiday Weekend Ends in Head-On Tragedy." The photo was signed "J. J. Luvs Ya!" Better days, Broady, better days, Amelia thought. He must have kept J. J. on his desk, since Amelia could see no spot for her on the crowded wall.

The scene was a macabre version of *This Is Your Life*, the walls of the office paneled with framed photographs, floor to ceiling, black and white, and yellowed, as if they had been left out in the limelight too long. They chronicled the life Broady manufactured for himself. Here hung a younger, horn-rimmed version, intruding on the private dinner conversation of a couple, featured players from that year's Academy Award winning picture. In that movie they gave rather undistinguished performances, but here, hanging on this warehouse wall thirty years later, they appeared every bit as talented as their more celebrated wall-mates. They looked just as stunned and embarrassed as the others. Who is this guy? they seemed to be saying through clenched teeth and forced grins.

"Remember these two?" Amelia asked Spiegal.

He looked away from his notes to glance at the photo. "No, I'm sorry. Were they friends of yours?"

"Oh, no. There's no reason why you would recognize them." In the upper right-hand corner of the autobiographical archives, in a dimestore metal frame, stared a puzzled Cary Grant, a bewildered Dyan Cannon.

"Marvelous people," Broady would enthuse. "A marvelous couple. But Grant couldn't take the pressure . . . if you know what I mean." Broady's creepy innuendos never ended. If you pressed the point, he'd tell you, in strictest confidence, the whole true story according to Broady. In fact, he would tell it to you whether you pressed or not.

Toward the bottom of the wall, hanging slightly off kilter, Mr. Jerry Broady popped unexpectedly into a frame with Frank Sinatra, Dean Martin and their then-current wives.

"You just slip around the other side of the table, Solly. They're wonderful friends of mine, as you know," Amelia could almost see him shellacking the lie with a smile, "but I don't want to disturb their dinner." The flash captured the crooners blinking, taken completely by surprise or Mr. Broady surely would have been decked, as he should have been.

Amelia remembered the roly-poly Solly. There had to be a Solly, an accomplice to record Broady's exploits, but he's never identified, the Boswell of Mr. Jerry Broady's self-proclaimed "very prestigious career."

"Solly Steinman was the photographer, Broady's sidekick in the beginning," Amelia said. Solly would be happy to hear that Broady was dead. Solly had been blackballed from every studio and nightclub in Hollywood for the part he played in Broady's photographic claims to fame. Broady suffered immediate and complete amnesia, called Solly a paparazzi, a sneak-thief of privacy, as though the shutterbug had acted alone. Solly should have killed him then, Amelia thought, but maybe it had taken him this long to work up the nerve.

"I suppose he should be told, too," Spiegal said, as though Amelia were making up a guest list for a memorial service.

The crime scene made Amelia world-weary, regretful of a life spent treading rumors. As a rookie reporter in the 'forties, she had been assigned the Hollywood beat because she was a woman and all the real reporting beats had been promised to the fighting men mustering out of the war. She took what she could get and depended on her talent and drive to get her out of the gossip ghetto.

Amelia earned a reputation as a fair and professional reporter. She treated her assignments with the same respect a Washington correspondent would give the White House. Amelia was an honorable woman; an excellent reporter, but she never left the backstage beat and she had

Mr. Jerry Broady to thank for that. Here on Broady's walls was a record of her life as well as his, although, as eyes and ears for the mighty *Times*, her name had been at the top of guest lists to cocktail parties, awards dinners and premiers that Broady crashed or hitched himself into via dates with the script girls and stunt doubles he promised to make famous. Amelia remembered the slight scandals that Broady started after each star-studded event.

She studied a picture of a serene-looking couple lost in each other's adoration. They had been oblivious to the arrival of a third in their dinner party—here's Jerry! Click! That photograph had been instrumental in ending two marriages. Four more with good reason to want Broady dead. Amelia caught a glimpse of herself in the background and winced at the black bouffant chiffon she had worn to that dinner. The women, including herself, had lacquered their hair into beehives and were heavily made up with flapping false lashes and jewel-colored eyelids that showed up as panda black circles in this picture. They looked like a bunch of tough babes by today's standards, but they had been glamorous then, hadn't they? Amelia could not be sure.

She pulled her half-glasses out of her purse, wanting a closer look at the misbegotten photo gallery: Jerry Broady in a Nehru jacket, neatly scalped by the camera's lens, leered into a frame shared by two jet-setting superstars of the time. Amelia remembered the evening. Jerry Broady had been insulted when the actress told him precisely what she thought of his tactics. Smarmy strong-arm, is what the woman accurately named them. Broady, in turn, told everybody that the woman had a history of psychiatric problems. Unstable, he had called her. She was a difficult star. It was the kind of gossip the movie moguls wanted to hear. It gave them good reason not to use her. The woman left for Europe shortly thereafter; she never worked in this country again. Motive for murder? Amelia thought so.

To Broady the actress's expatriation had been the ultimate demonstration of his power. He never stopped bad-mouthing the girl, even after she was long gone. From that time on his villainy grew in direct proportion to the number of doors that were finally opened, albeit reluctantly. Hollywood supported a rather nervous constellation of stars in those days. They could not afford to say no. Broady used his blackmail to extort smiles from people who were sneering inside. It was worth a lot to a man like him to keep those sneers covered up. Amelia imagined even Jerry Broady's thick skin was capable of cringing.

Amelia had worked her way down the wall until she was in an uncomfortable, knee-wrenching crouch she was quite sure she could not get out of gracefully; but here, at this rat's eye level was a picture she would not have wanted to miss. It was a standard issue studio publicity shot of Johnny Collins, circa 1948. It was autographed, "I guess we've had some fun together. Your old friend, Johnny." Amelia knew Broady had signed the photo himself, he was no friend of Johnny's. Johnny was a star, but in the Amelia Crater Story he had been cast in a cameo.

Amelia had been ready to see her by-line go big time with the publication of her story on a major studio shake-up. She had had in her possession a damning handwritten memo from the desk of the studio's president and on-the-record quotes from impeccable sources. First-rate reporting, a career-making story, but before it broke, she had made the mistake of looking the wrong way at Jerry Broady. She never knew what word or action was escalated in his mind from unintended slight to slander, but snubbed, he set out to get even. He started the rumor that Amelia was sleeping with Collins, matinee idol and subject of some of her more favorable reviews and interviews.

Broady had put on his death-mask grin and lied about Amelia to people who wanted to damage her credibility — those studio executives whose careers would crumble if her shake-up story hit the newsstands. No one ever suggested that she had compromised herself or the newspaper, at least not publicly. No one, in truth, cared with whom she slept, even in 1949. She never had the opportunity to defend herself because no one ever accused her of anything. It had been carried out *sotto voce* by studio bosses who did not want an investigative reporter in the Hollywood press corps and by newspaper editors who did not want an ambitious woman moving up through their ranks. How convenient the right rumor can be. Johnny Collins was the salve to their collective consciences for killing her story. It withered and died on an editor's desk along with her shot at a front-page career.

Not without difficulty, despite Detective Spiegal's assistance, Amelia got back to her feet. She knew Spiegal thought she was grieving a fallen friend, her lost youth, and he was half right. Amelia regarded her younger self with disdain. What a fool she had been to value dignity over her own self-worth. Amelia had recognized Broady's handiwork from the start of her undoing, but what was a reporter to do? Journalistic objectivity disallowed a smear campaign, the tenets of femininity frowned upon fist fights, and Amelia had feared that Broady was capable of worse than he had already done to her. What a very killable guy he had been, and lucky, too, that Amelia's personal code of ethics did not condone revenge. If she had only known then how long life was going to be, and how small a part Broady would play in hers, she could have found the courage to take him on at the time, forced his accusations out into the open where she could challenge them. She had to laugh. These days she needed eyeglasses for everything but hindsight.

"Ms. Crater, I want you to know that we will do everything in our power to find your friend's killer." He was showing her a courtesy, waiting when he should have been rushing off to a new shooting scene. But she was convinced that there was more to this story than robbery-murder, some piece of the past not accounted for, and she needed Spiegal's solicitude for a few moments more.

"You've been very kind and patient," Amelia said. "I'm sure I've been a nuisance this afternoon. I know that you will do your utmost to solve this case." Amelia stood behind the desk, looking for what? A name spelled out in bloody script? Broady had made quite a mess of the desk, apparently gunned down while reading a newspaper. It would be too much to hope that he had been perusing her column when he met his end. The paper was *Daily Variety*, an issue two days old, the slick pages, stained first with coffee, now by blood, opened to a two-column story on the controversy over colorization of classic black-and-white films. Next to it ran a story on the dedication of the Susan Janson Women's Clinic at Cedars-Sinai Hospital, which Amelia had attended at the personal invitation of movie tycoon Stanley Janson, the clinic's sole benefactor. Hardly the social event of the season, and Broady's interest in young women certainly did not include matters philanthropic. Slightly farther down the page Amelia saw a tiny black-bordered ad that must have caught Broady's eye: "You Are On Your Way To Hollywood Stardom! Call Broady Entertainment Enterprises Today." Then the phone number. She wondered if people ever called the number, and how much malarkey they were subjected to when they got through to Broady. The telephone was the greatest instrument for lying ever invented, Amelia thought. It was so easy to make yourself misunderstood.

"I'm finished here," she said. "Thank you again for your patience." Speigal insisted on escorting her to her car. Graciously, he supported her elbow and tried to reassure her that they were hot on the trail of the gunman. He opened the door of her Bonneville convertible, a car she had bought twenty years ago because it matched a shade of lipstick she wore at the time. It was now an elegant relic, much like herself.

"Beautiful automobile," Spiegal said. "But I bet it's a pain to park."

"I pull out my press card and park wherever I like. Just like the police."

"That's right," Spiegal said. "Okay. Take care of yourself and rest easy about your friend. Justice will be done."

Amelia thanked him again and sent him back to the scene of the crime. She fixed her lipstick in the rear-view mirror, put on sunglasses and steered the convertible out onto Cahuenga Boulevard. This was the tattered edge of Hollywood the civic beautification plan had not reached, and never would. Packs of cast-off, mongrel children had made this turf their own, scrawling graffiti across the streamlined art deco buildings that had been the heart of filmdom in Amelia's heyday. Today the past rose up from the ruins and chased her all the way to the freeway.

Broady's artifacts held the answer, of that Amelia was sure. She only had to sort the facts from the meaningless memorabilia. Dean Martin, Frank Sinatra, Dyan Cannon, Johnny Collins et al., were faces too famous and lives too closely scrutinized to suffer more than momentary discomfort from Broady's exploits. Solly Steinman, the photographer, had plenty of motive, but not enough time. Amelia was sure that Broady had outlived him. The expatriate actress was now Baroness So-and-So or Viscountess Such-and-Such, at home on the Cote d'Azur and far removed from the concerns of Hollywood's back-biting box-office royalty. But who was the comely J. J.? Amelia imagined her picture on Broady's desk as he sat checking to see if *Variety* had spelled his name right. Then, as though Amelia were sitting there beside him, she saw his killer walk through the office door. At last Amelia could make sense of Broady's downfall and his death. He had one enemy who could not forgive and forget. Someone who suffered a loss that has no half-life, but burns white hot forever.

By 1963, Broady had a client list glitzy with pseudo-celebrities, game-show hosts, soap opera stars, showgirls and starlets. He had a house in Bel Air, an office on Sunset Boulevard, and enemies who knew Broady was unscrupulous, therefore unstoppable. His name made more hate lists than the Hay's Office and Joe McCarthy combined.

Then on a flint-dry September night, Jacqueline Jacaranda—J. J. as in J. J. Luvs Ya—died in the ladies' room of the Sun Goddess A-Go-Go in Malibu, hemorrhaged from a back-alley abortion. The unfortunate young woman would have filled a coroner's drawer in ignominious anonymity had she been Miss Jacaranda. In fact, she was Susan Janson, only daughter, only child of Stanley Janson. The press descended, their interest clearly prurient, since in the early 'sixties that kind of story was unfit to print in family newspapers. Grief-mongering was not in Amelia's repertoire of journalistic tools. Refusing to trivialize the family's heart-break, she allowed for a decent amount of mourning before phoning Janson to express her sympathy and get a quote from him for a cautionary piece her editor had assigned on "The Starlet System: How High is the Price of Success?"

"My baby had such guts," he said. "She was not going to let daddy make her a star. She did everything on her own. She was so proud when she'd get an audition, and I was proud of her. Now I get no rest. I cannot rest until my little girl's killer is named. You can understand, Amelia, a father's love."

Amelia understood.

"If I ever find out who is responsible for her slaughter, he will be bloodied, too," Janson said with the certainty of a man who passes judgment every day. "You know more about what goes on in this town than anyone. I would be thankful for any help you might give me, Amelia."

There were dozens of Dr. Take-Care-Of-Its around town, as easy to find as bootleg booze during Prohibition. Maybe Susan had not wanted daddy to know what kind of talent she employed to win her auditions. Perhaps she had a kind, loving suitor who wanted her to surrender her career and marry him. Most likely Stanley Janson would never find a target at which to aim his grief.

"You know I would do anything I could to help. Perhaps my story will bring forth new information on the case." Amelia recalled with startling clarity the telephone conversation that had taken place more than twenty years before, as though she had finally tuned into the correct frequency. Today she understood the meaning behind the words they had exchanged. She had said, "If we help only one girl avoid the dangers Susan faced, we will have accomplished much. I think we can help each other. If I could just impose upon you to verify some information regarding your daughter."

"Yes, Amelia. Certainly." She had interpreted his eager tone as generosity of spirit, his desire to help.

"Susan was managed by Broady Entertainment Enterprises, wasn't she?"

Janson had been silent for a time, a few moments only. Amelia had thought it was too painful for him to discuss his daughter, her career. Now she knew that Stanley Janson thought he had his answer: What kind of man would take a nineteen-year-old girl to a slaughterhouse? A man like Jerry Broady. For Janson, it finally all fit. He had continued their discussion, giving perfunctory answers to Amelia's polite questions. Broady's name never came up again, but by the next day Broady's career crucifixion was underway. Had Amelia been paying attention she would have seen that his demise was swift, but far from painless, as one by one the power-brokers who had long enough suffered Broady's insinuations fell upon this absolute proof of his wickedness and whispered it from rooftops all over town. Broady had to have known of what he was accused, the picture of J. J. was evidence of that, but the deed was too heinous and Janson too powerful for Broady to attempt a defense.

The Bonneville barreled onto the Hollywood Freeway. Justice, Detective Spiegal had promised. Amelia would have to ask whose version of justice he had in mind. Had an unflinching Stanley Janson pulled the trigger, believing he was taking final payment on a debt that had not been satisfactorily settled by Broady's ruination? Whose justice would be served by imprisoning him for the deed? Amelia recalled Janson's words from the hospital dedication ceremony only a few days earlier: "This is the good I can do in the memory of my daughter." If someone had to pay for Susan Janson's death, who better than Broady, who had never done good by anyone?

If Spiegal charged some hyped-up kid with the killing, Amelia realized she would have to come forward with her suspicions, though she felt confident that occasion would not occur. Nothing against Spiegal, but Amelia knew the L.A.P.D.'s record in solving such cases was not as spotless as, say, the Mounties'. Until that time, Amelia would keep her own counsel on this one. After all, her accusations would be nothing more than idle supposition, unsubstantiated rumor, mere gossip that would never stand as evidence in a court of law.

As far as journalistic integrity goes, her professional position on the murder of Mr. Jerry Broady was this: Whodunit? Who cares? Now she could just lean back, let the wind blow through her hair, and enjoy the feeling of smug justification, gratification, even out-and-out jubilation at the small, naive, unwitting part she had played in turning Broady's most deadly weapon, the whispered word, against him. Driving west, starting to catch the scent of the sea in the air, she knew there was no chance of Broady rising grinning from the grave to add a sad epilogue to the Amelia Crater Story. The ending would be upbeat: Amelia in a dress the color of her car, to go with her favorite shade of lipstick, the sunset straight ahead.

Film at Eleven

ANNA ASHWOOD-COLLINS

"*I*'ve had worse days," Abby Benson muttered as she stared at the photos on the wall, graphically showing the bodies of two murdered homeless women. Bludgeoned to death, limp bundles of bloody broken bones.

"I don't want this assignment," she said as she bleakly contemplated the chief of detectives. "I don't feel good. I think I'm coming down with something."

"Ridiculous. Have a cold on your own time." He held up a beefy hand to forestall her comment. "Only joking. After this one you can have a week off, lie in the sun."

"If I'm still alive," the Queen of Disguise snapped. Abby, tapped by the chief of detectives while she was still in the police academy seven years ago, was famous for her disguises. Undercover assignments had taken her from high society to the warrens of the homeless under the streets of New York.

She pulled out a cigarette and placed it on the desk. She stared at it.

"How many you down to now?" the chief asked.

"Four a day except in emergencies."

"Emergencies?"

"Yeh. Remember ten-day-old bodies?"

"Well, yes. But getting back to our current problem, we've had two bag ladies killed in the past month. And if that isn't bad enough, Jessica Jarvis is going undercover as a bag lady to see how the homeless survive on these mean streets."

"So? I don't like News Scene and I don't like her. Every chance she gets she takes a pop at the police and she plays fast and loose with the facts. The other media people call her 'Hit and Run.' She goes for the sensational, the shallow."

"I know, but can you imagine the field day the press will have if something happens to her on the subway?"

Abby grinned. "Film at eleven."

As if on cue, Jessica Jarvis flung open the chief's door and strode to his desk. "How dare you interfere in a news operation!"

"I beg your pardon." The chief stood. "What are you talking about?"

"My producer just told me that you're providing an armed guard while I'm on undercover assignment. No way. I don't want your Neanderthals getting between me and the street people. I want the real story."

Abby enjoyed the chief's discomfort as she studied Jarvis. Her long black hair and snapping black eyes emphasized the newswoman's classic beauty. She made Abby feel small, homely and inferior.

Jarvis pointed at Abby. "Who is this person?"

"My secretary," the chief said.

Abby raised an eyebrow and asked sweetly, "Would you like some coffee, Ms. Jarvis? I so enjoy your programs. I can hardly wait for your special on the homeless."

The chief glared at her. "I don't need you any more, Ms. Benson."

●

The chief called Abby early the next morning. "Sorry to get you up, but Jarvis is going out tonight. Len Rogers, her cameraman, just called me. She's starting in the subway. He'll give us an exact location later. Get ready to put on your glad rags."

Abby groaned and coughed. "I feel worse. Can't you get somebody else? Besides, she saw me yesterday and she might recognize me."

"Not a chance. Your own mother wouldn't recognize you when you're done. Stay by the phone today. And Abby, whatever you do, don't let anything happen to that woman."

"Maybe she'll get run over by a train," Abby muttered as she hung up the phone and reached for her first cigarette. Puffing away, she looked in the mirror. Her cold already made her look down-and-out. Red-rimmed eyes, red nose, bags under her eyes.

The chief called back at four o'clock. "Penn Station at eight. The A train. I assume you can spot her by yourself."

"Yeh, I just look for a bag lady with a makeup artist, hair stylist, agent, cameraman—did I leave anybody out?"

"Don't let anything happen to her."

"I'll do my best. I feel worse," Abby said into a dead phone.

●

The old woman was a filthy mumbling apparition as she lurched through Penn Station. She clutched a paper-covered bottle in her left hand. A faded New York Mets knit cap was pulled down to her eyebrows. Stringy gray hair straggled out at the sides. Thick glasses obscured her eyes. Several layers of clothes added the illusion of an extra thirty pounds.

Abby's eyes were constantly in motion behind the thick clear lens. She noted the regulars. Her eyes rested briefly on the black man who always sat in a corner facing the wall, a paper cup behind him in which people occasionally dropped coins.

The Mayor of Penn Station's netherworld, a middle-aged Viet Nam veteran, greeted Abby. A former lawyer, he had lost everything to the drug habit he brought back as a war souvenir. "Hey, Queenie, you been sick again?"

Head down, Abby mumbled, "Yeh, flu."

He whispered, "Be careful, I hear the mayor's ordered another roust. Toss us all out on Thirty-fourth Street or herd us into those shelters with the animals."

"I'll take the A train like the Duke said," Abby mumbled, drifting away.

She shambled past the token clerk, who sighed and looked the other way as Abby entered the exit gate. Abby hunkered down near the turnstile to watch for Jessica Jarvis. She choked off a laugh when she saw a bag lady putting a token in the turnstile.

Jessica Jarvis was dressed in bag lady chic. The rags were a little too well-coordinated, a little too clean, and she lacked the proper aroma as she sidled up to Abby and said, "I'm new here. How long have you been on the streets?"

Abby made a strangling noise and edged closer to Jessica, who pulled back when Abby's odor assailed her. Abby thrust the bottle at her. "Have a swig, sweetie," she rasped. "You and me kin be buddies. I'll show you the best spots."

An A train roared into the station. Jessica leaped for the nearest door while Abby shuffled to the next car. Hope I've scared her off, she thought. I just want to keep an eye on her, not be her best buddy. Abby hacked and coughed. Nearby riders moved away.

Nothing happened that night. Jessica left the subway system at midnight, discreetly followed by Abby until the policewoman realized the TV star was headed for her Park Avenue apartment.

Abby sighed. "I should be so lucky." She turned and headed west to a single-room occupancy hotel on Forty-second Street where the chief kept a room for the select few of his people who worked the streets. Abby prayed nobody was using it.

Abby woke up a little before noon and called the chief. "Can you get somebody else? My cold is really bad." She coughed and wheezed into the phone.

"Please Abby, just try to hang on. I don't think she'll last much longer. Her cameraman called and said Her Nibs is appalled by the way street people smell. She mentioned a particularly pungent bag lady. You?"

"Yup. Garlic works every time. She could hardly wait to get away from me. Where's she going tonight?"

"Grand Central."

"Terrific. Grand Central is a big place. Give me a hint."

"Wait at the Forty-second Street entrance."

Shortly after eight o'clock Abby shuffled down Forty-second Street, cursing the arctic February wind and her worsening cold. She ached all over. Gratefully, she entered the warm station and slumped down in the hallway. She had changed her rags, discarded the thick glasses and the gray wig. Instead, she wore a garish blond wig topped by a faded Yankee baseball cap. She clutched the whiskey bottle filled with sugary tea to her chest.

Jesssica swept into the station like the leading lady in a play about bag ladies. Abby shuffled along behind her through the tunnel to the No. 7 train platform.

Hearing a commotion behind her, Abby turned in time to see two teenage boys slug a middle-aged man carrying a large shoulder bag. He slumped to his knees. The thugs kicked him and wrenched the bag out of his hands. Abby glimpsed a minicam unit.

"Oh, no," she groaned, "Jessica's cameraman." She started to go to his rescue when she realized that Jessica, unaware that her cameraman had been mugged, was confidently boarding the train to Flushing Main Street. She would be totally unprotected. A vision of the chief's angry face spurred Abby into action. She sprinted for the last car and wedged herself in the closing door. It snapped open, tumbling her inside.

She walked through the train until she found Jessica, who was sitting bolt upright like a proper lady. Abby shook her head, suppressing a grin. Bag ladies slouch, Miss High 'n Mighty, she thought to herself.

Abby sprawled in a corner seat. Ah, at least twenty minutes of heat, she thought contentedly, figuring that Jessica would stay on to the end of the line in Flushing. Abby dozed between stations, opening one eye at each stop.

At the Shea Stadium stop, Jessica unexpectedly exited at the last minute, leaving Abby behind, pounding on the closing doors. She shrugged. "What can happen to her in just a few minutes? I'll catch the return train."

Jessica looked up and down the platform in bewilderment. "Len, Len," she called, "where are you?" Her voice echoed eerily in the silence. "He must've left through another exit," she assured herself. She hurried down the ramp, drawn by the lights of the token seller's booth. She whipped out her compact and checked her makeup before she rapped on the booth's glass. "Have you seen a tall man carrying a shoulder bag?" she asked.

The token seller glanced up from his book. He wrinkled his nose in disgust. "Ain't seen nobody."

Jessica snapped, "My good man . . ." before she remembered her disguise. Len's probably downstairs waiting for me, she reassured herself, as she walked down the stairs. She stared up at the ominous shadow of the stadium.

"Len," she called again. Fearfully, she stared into the shadows. Pulling her rags closer and clutching her shopping bag tighter, Jessica shivered, partly from the cold and partly from fear.

"I'll wait for him upstairs, she decided, turning toward the stairs.

Suddenly, a hand reached out of the darkness and slid over her mouth, and she was jerked off the stairs into the darkness beneath the staircase.

The stench of urine-soaked clothes and rotting teeth gagged her. Heavy breathing rasped in her ear.

"You're prettier than most, dearie. Got a few pennies for Big Al?" His hands mauled her body. She struggled and attempted to scream before he twisted her around and slugged her.

●

Abby boarded the waiting Manhattan-bound train. The doors stayed open. "Come on, come on, let's move this thing out," she shouted as she pounded on the conductor's door. Her fellow passengers nervously moved away from her. Finally, the doors closed and the train roared out of the station, across the Roosevelt Bridge into the Shea stop in a matter of minutes.

She sprinted down the ramp to the token booth. "Didja see a bag woman go out this way?"

The clerk looked up from his book. "Whad they do, turn Shea into a shelter for you old broads?"

Abby slammed her badge against the glass. "Don't be a wise guy."

"That way," he pointed to the stairs.

Abby paused at the top of the stairs to scan the area. Crying from below alerted her. She tiptoed down the stairs.

"Please don't, please don't, I have money. Lots of money," whimpered Jessica as the man ripped at her clothes.

Geez, he's huge, Abby thought as she grabbed his shoulder and yelled, "Freeze, police!"

Suddenly, he straightened up and flung her backward. Her head banged against a concrete pillar. The wig absorbed some of the shock. Groggily, she tugged at her gun, but it snagged on her ragged sweater.

The man leaped on top of her and started beating at her head. Abby struggled desperately, twisting and turning, protecting her head with her right forearm. Still clutching the bottle of tea in her left hand, she used the last of her strength to smash it into his temple. He collapsed on top of her.

Abby pushed his body aside. She shook her head to clear it and winced at the throbbing pain. "Whoo, you smell worse than I do, Mac," she muttered as she frisked him, coming up with a switchblade and a few coins. She cuffed him before she looked for Jessica.

"You okay?" Abby asked as she leaned over Jessica, who was mumbling to herself. "What'd you say?" Abby asked, worrying that Jessica was badly injured and hysterical.

Jessica pushed her away. "Don't bother me. I'm preparing my copy. What a story!"

Abby leaped up. "You almost got killed. *I* almost got killed. Your cameraman has been mugged and God only knows if he's all right, and all you can think of is your story. God help us, lady!"

•

The chief ushered Abby into his den. He studied her. "That black eye will look great on the beach. By the way, nice collar. That creep confessed to killing the two homeless women. He wandered here from Chicago. Probably wanted back there, too."

Abby winced as she shook her head. "I was lucky. He was some big bruiser."

The chief smiled at her. "Sit down. You're just in time for the eleven o'clock news and Jessica Jarvis's story."

"No thanks, I lived it." Abby lit her fifth cigarette of the day and glanced at the screen. Jessica, still clad in her bag lady chic, her face bruised and scraped, announced, "Tonight, I was the victim of the seamy underside of this city. . . ."

Abby reached for the doorknob.

"Don't you want to see what she has to say about you?" the chief asked.

Abby smiled. "She already said it to me. I quote, 'You stink, and why are you interfering in my story.' I'll send you a postcard from Miami Beach."

No Handicap

JUDITH POST

Colleen was working late, sketching out a new ad campaign, one Dan would appreciate. In a manner of speaking, they were both busy at the same thing this time. His narc team was trying to keep drugs off the street and so was she. She glanced at the clock. Almost six. Dan had promised to pick her up at five, but if he had a new lead, who knew when he'd show up? Everyone else had left the office over an hour ago. Friday night flight, scurrying to hearth or bars, depending largely upon whether they were married or not.

Colleen and Dan were very much married. Three years of fairly liberated bliss. Marrying a cop takes a strong woman, and not many were more feisty or independent than Colleen. Of course, she had to be, or she'd have given way to self-pity long ago when her parents had wanted to smother her with love to make up for her loss. A natural reaction, but Colleen would have none of it.

Sure, it had been tough at first. For a nine-year-old girl to go to bed with a fever, listening to her mother offering soothing words, and then to wake up to a silent world, was no picnic. At first, she'd thought people were mouthing things, not using their voices—and then she realized that her ears didn't work. The nerve endings had burned clear through, leaving her deaf.

For a while, things were pretty bleak. She denied it, fought it, mourned, raved—but finally came to terms with it. At nine years old, she picked herself up, dusted herself off, and got on with life, accepted reality. Being deaf couldn't be altered, but her attitude could; and attitude, she learned, was the make-it-or-break-it difference.

She was going to make it, by God!

She took deaf classes and learned to use sign language. She lip-read so well most people didn't realize she was deaf. She formed a tight network of deaf and hearing friends and refused to be pitied or made fun of. She'd always been a tomboy, and it didn't bother her one bit to punch a smart-aleck in the mouth at recess time.

Concentration came easy. Without sound, there were few distractions. She excelled at school, then at college, graduating with an offer from a top ad agency.

Meeting Dan had been a fluke. She was speeding, as usual, roaring along the interstate on her way home to visit her parents. He'd followed her in his squad car, siren blaring, red lights flashing, before she glanced in her rear-view mirror and noticed. When she pulled over and rolled down her window, he stomped to the car, absolutely furious.

"I've been following you for over a mile!" he fumed. "Why didn't you pull to the side of the road?"

"I'm sorry. I didn't hear you."

"Damn stereos," he mumbled, pulling a ticket pad from his back pocket. "Probably had it blasting full volume."

She said nothing.

Looking down, he asked, "Name?"

She sat, waiting.

"Name?" he repeated, pen poised over the paper.

Nothing.

Looking up, fighting to control his temper, he said clearly and distinctly, "Do you have a name?"

"Colleen Callahan."

"May I see your driver's license?"

She handed it to him. The word *Deaf* leaped from its shiny surface.

"Oh, hell," Dan said. He looked up frowning, almost apologetic, then caught the smug smile on her face.

She was really pretty, he thought, with platinum hair and dark brown eyes—and deaf. Probably spoiled. Pampered. Used to getting her own way.

"Stay put," he said. "I'm going to check this out."

He went back to his squad car and radioed in. A few minutes later, he returned to Colleen, looking smug himself. "You have a rack of warning tickets deep enough to bury most people. You always get off because you can't hear."

Her black eyes sparkled. Temper or humor? he wondered. But she said nothing.

"Well, I don't think being deaf gives you the right to turn your car into a lethal weapon. This time, you pay your dues."

He wrote out a ticket and handed it to her.

"What's your name?" she asked.

"Dan Bristow. Why? Are you going to report me?"

"I like you. Can I take you to dinner Friday night?"

First he eyed her, surprised. Then a slow smile lit his face. "Sure, policemen are usually hungry. But I'll pick *you* up. I'd rather work vice than let you drive."

And somehow, from that inauspicious beginning, the two of them grew deeply attracted to each other. Attracted enough so that a short four months later, they tied the knot. A good knot, too. One that a boy scout could be proud of, because three years later, it was still looped tight.

●

Colleen watched the clock tick past six, six-thirty, and finally six forty-five. Dan still hadn't come to take her home.

At seven, frowning over an ad of giant sunglasses with a large *No* printed across one corner, she became aware of footsteps padding into the room. Dan, at last, had arrived.

She motioned to her poster-sized drawing. "What do you think?"

He stared at the bold colored campaign. "Pretty good. Jackson Carlisle should like it, even if he'd rather take drugs than wage war against them. Judge Nagel came up with a good idea, making a celebrity pay off his probation by going public with his problem."

She nodded. "Kids idolize TV stars. Once their heroes give one-minute ads about the downside of drugs, maybe the message will sink in."

"And maybe the heroes can stay clean for a change."

"How's your case going?" she asked, as they made their way through the office.

"It's not. All dead-ends. And I mean *dead*. Another kid bit the dust this morning, only twelve years old. Crack's cheap on the street, so there's a supplier, but we can't even find the pushers. No one's talking."

They walked to the car and Dan opened the passenger door for her. "How does Joe's sound tonight?" he asked. "I could use a cold one."

"Anything's good I don't have to cook."

They drove to the old neighborhood where Dan had grown up and pulled over in front of a corner tavern. Joe Pequinot served fish 'n chips every Friday, all you could eat. As they pushed past the men, elbow-deep at the bar watching the game on Joe's TV, Gracie Merton spotted them and waved them to an empty table.

"Just cleaned this one," she said, slapping water glasses and silverware on the formica top. "What do you want, the Friday night special? Joe's wavin' at ya, Dan. Wants to see ya."

"Order for me, will you?" he asked Colleen, then drifted away. It was a fact of life. Get him in a crowd and he always ditched her; had to stop to say Hi and left her sitting alone.

Taking a deep draw from the beer Gracie brought her, Colleen studied the crowd. A mixed group. The older regulars, dressed in polyester pants and white shoes, were waiting for the first snowflakes to send them scurrying to Florida. The younger crowd was poorer and louder. The neighborhood was changing. In a few years, it would be too rough to trek to on Friday nights.

Gracie brought two plates heaped with fish and chips. Dumping ketchup in a red heap, Colleen dipped a fry, then searched the bar for Dan. Catching his eye, she signalled that the food had arrived. Fingers flying, he signed he'd be a few minutes more.

A young kid, cheeks and chin bristling with whiskers, a key dangling on a chain through his ear, caught their exchange and turned to stare at her. "Hey, you're some looker," he said. "What's the matter? Your old man give you the slip?"

"He'll be here in a minute," Colleen said.

"What was the stuff with the fingers?" he asked. "You got some secret code?"

"It's sign language," she explained. "I'm deaf."

"What? You can't hear?"

She nodded.

"Eh," he called to two men nearby. "This woman can't hear."

They turned to stare; and laughing, the kid went to join them. The three made a perfect trio, she thought, all sporting long stringy hair, leather jackets, faded jeans. Forgetting her, they leaned into the center of the table, absorbed in earnest discussion.

She read their lips shamelessly. What could three young men be so serious about? Girls, maybe? One of their motorcycles had developed a serious cough? They barely looked the legal age.

The tall one with dishwater blond hair drooping in straggly clumps around his face, had a cigarette dangling from his lips. She gave up trying to catch his words. The second man—the one she'd been lucky enough to meet—turned his head toward the others, only showing his profile. No help there. But the third was choosing his words carefully. He was no cinch, since he slurred and favored contractions, but Colleen could still make out what he said.

"You got that, Jimmy Boy?" he asked. "We ain't got room for no slip-ups. Ricardo'll be on Pearl Street at eleven-fifteen with the stuff. His boys'll be leavin' the Y carryin' gym bags. Every bag stuffed full of crack. You'll be drivin' down Main and your car'll stall a block from the Y. His boys'll spot ya, come to give ya a hand. Open the trunk to get a flashlight, full of bills instead o' batteries, and the swap's done. We'll have the stuff on the street first thing in the mornin'. Even before school starts."

Jimmy Boy nodded his head.

The speaker grabbed him by the shirt collar. "And one more thing. Ya do things *my* way, with no problems, hear? Or I tell the man. Jaycee don't like no little inconveniences."

Jimmy Boy's head looked like a yo-yo, it bobbed up and down so fast.

"Good. Then that's settled." The leader and the blond stood to leave, followed by Jimmy a few minutes later.

Colleen looked for Dan. He was swapping football yarns with Joe, something both could do for hours. She gave him a wave, calling him to the table.

"Gotta go," Dan said, "or the fish won't be the only thing fried around here. My goose will be cooked, too."

He hurried to join her and searched for his tartar sauce. Too late—she'd already taken it. "Didn't mean to yack so long, but you know how it is," he apologized.

She knew, all right, but let it pass.

While they ate, she told him about the three young toughs.

"Are you sure?" Dan asked. "At the Y on Main, at eleven-fifteen?"

"That's what he said, the one facing me. The second kid with the cigarette in his mouth never said a word. Jimmy's the one doing the job."

"A tall kid, big and lanky?" Dan asked. "Has blond hair that's never been washed?"

"That's the one with the cigarette."

"I know him. Rents himself out as a bodyguard. I'm going to make a quick call so the narc team can case out the Y and get some men in position."

Colleen watched Dan cross to the pay phone in the back of the restaurant. She signalled Gracie for seconds and another beer.

"So how did it go?" she asked when Dan returned.

"Fred will have a team waiting at the Y. When the deal goes down, we'll be ready."

They hurried through the rest of their meal, Dan anxious to take her home, then join Fred and his team.

●

It was early morning before the light in the living room switched on, signalling Dan was home. They'd wired it to turn on when anyone entered the apartment. Colleen felt his footsteps coming down the hall. "Success?" she called.

Dan sat on the edge of the bed and wrapped her in a bear hug, then gave her a wet smack on the lips. "You're incredible, Snoopy Sleuth. Poor Jimmy Boy and his friends are all caged, and a trunkload of crack is sitting downtown."

"So you caught them?"

"First we got Jimmy and Ricardo's crew in front of the Y. Then we picked up Ricardo, while Fred snagged Vincent and Bobby."

"Vincent and Bobby?" she asked.

"The two from the bar."

"What about Jaycee?"

Dan frowned. "No such person. Maybe someone will sing and we'll pull in more."

She glanced at the clock. Two-thirty. "You look tired. It's Saturday. Get in bed. We'll sleep in."

•

By Monday morning, their lives were back to routine. Dan drove her to the office and dropped her off. "I'll be here on time tonight," he promised, pulling away.

Colleen worked on her ad layouts with fresh zeal. The weekend's escapade had pumped new adrenalin into the "Say NO" campaign.

When she'd finished all of the art work, she made a phone call to Jackson Carlisle's publicist. "The rough drafts are done for Mr. Carlisle's approval," she said. "I'm sending copies over. We should go over ideas for his script soon."

"Mr. Carlisle will get back to you," the publicist promised. "He's in wardrobe right now and can't be reached, but when the ads get here, I'll make sure he sees them."

Colleen watched the words dart across the base of her telephone—a special model for the deaf. Fair enough, she decided, Jackson Carlisle could look the campaign over at his convenience, and she could take a break. It was close to quitting time, and she'd skipped lunch, trying to finish things up. She arranged to have the ads delivered to Carlisle right away and headed over to the coffee machine.

Travis and Alec were there, both a little down in the mouth about a new wine promotion they couldn't get off the ground.

"Brainstorm with us a second," they pleaded. "Just to get the juices flowing again."

She stayed longer than she planned before returning to her office. The light on her telephone was blinking.

"Hello?"

"Colleen? It's J. C. here. Got the copy of your ads. They look great!" The words flew across the base of her phone. "Things are really coming together. I can work on a script with you later in the week. Is that soon enough?"

She stared at the print-out. "J. C.," she said aloud. "Initials, of course. . . ."

"What? What are you talking about?"

"Oh, nothing, really—just your name."

"My name? Hmmm—will the end of the week be okay with you?" She was thinking.

"Colleen? Are you still there?" Carlisle asked. "I made a couple of changes on the sunglasses poster. I could drop it off on my way home from the studio. Would that be okay?"

"I won't be here that long," she said. "I was just leaving."

"Already? You usually stay late."

"My husband's picking me up early."

"Your husband—he's a policeman, isn't he?" There was a pause. "Maybe I'll swing by and leave the poster at the desk."

When he hung up, she tried to call Dan.

"Sorry, he's not at the station," a desk sergeant said, "but I could try to radio him."

"No, he'll be here soon . . . it'll wait."

She tidied her desk, then walked to the parking garage. She didn't want to be in the office if Jackson Carlisle popped in. Leaning against a cement pillar, she waited for Dan. It was five-fifteen. She hoped he wouldn't be too late.

At five-thirty, a battered blue station wagon swung onto the fourth floor of the garage. Colleen glanced at it, then looked away. As it pulled to a stop, the door on the passenger's side swung open and a tall, thin man with thick gray hair and heavy glasses leaned across the seat. "Is this the Summit Parking Building?" he called.

Colleen couldn't see his lips well enough to read them, so she stepped closer to the car. In an instant, the man had hold of her arm and yanked her into the car. In the scuffle, his wig and glasses tumbled onto the front seat. Jackson Carlisle didn't care. Slamming her door, he spun the car and raced toward the down ramp. He took the exit curves quickly, discouraging her from trying to grab for the steering wheel.

Panic filled her as they sped toward the street.

They'd reached the ground exit when three squad cars blocked their way. Cursing violently, Carlisle jumped from the car and tried to make a run for it, but he was tackled by a policeman before he'd gone twenty feet.

Then Colleen's door was yanked open and strong arms pulled her from the seat.

"Are you all right?" Dan buried his face against her cheek.

Colleen clung to him for a moment, then asked, "How did you know?"

"The desk sergeant got me just after you'd called. When I looked at my watch, I knew I was going to be late. I tried to get in touch with you — but you'd already gone. I called Alec to see where you were. He checked your office for me and found a print-out from your telephone conversation with Carlisle. He read it all to me, plus the note you scribbled at the bottom of it."

After a few hard kisses, Dan sighed. "I always thought that marrying a policeman wasn't safe for you, but you know what? This time, it worked out pretty well. You'd have gotten yourself in trouble anyway, reading lips when you shouldn't. Having me around might be just what you need."

"What *I* need?" she asked. "How long would it have taken you to figure out that Carlisle was the man you were looking for?"

Dan smiled. "I've got to admit, you were a little ahead of me this time. The note you left on your desk is what clinched it: J. C.'s drug campaign is a bust."

Colleen nuzzled into him. "I'd say having *me* around is just what *you* need."

The Disappearing Diamond

HELEN AND LORRI CARPENTER

*E*mma Twiggs's excuse for making the perilous trek downtown on Wednesday afternoon was to extend a dinner invitation. It would have been less nerve-wracking to phone than to brave the crowded city, but Emma liked to visit Jim and Nancy. Her matchmaker's heart eagerly accepted the challenge of taming the adversarial sparks that flew between her private detective nephew and his secretary when they thought she wasn't looking. Besides, by presenting herself at the office in person, there was always the chance she'd get to assist with a case, or "intervene," as Jim liked to say.

I feel lucky today, Emma mused inwardly. She evaded the cab that threatened to run her down and entered the building without noticing the screech of tires, or the mugger who found out the hard way that nimble-footed elderly ladies weren't such easy marks.

"Unfortunately," Nancy informed her when she arrived on the top floor of the Galveston Building, "Jim is out of town for the rest of the week, at a private investigators' convention. I guess he forgot to tell you."

The unexpected news didn't deter Emma from extending the dinner invitation anyway. Then, on the pretext of freshening up while the younger woman finished for the day, she slipped into Jim's private office. Tiptoeing across the room, she sank into the plush leather chair and, with unrestrained pleasure, placed her feet on his desk.

Having accomplished the one thing she'd vowed to do if ever given the opportunity, she relaxed and leaned back to survey her nephew's

Excellence in Sleuthing awards through the gap between her sensible shoes. From this angle, the awards were highly impressive.

While she was inclining her head for a more advantageous view, she noticed the newspaper lying beside the telephone. The three-word headline immediately caught her eye: *Fox Diamond Stolen!* Emma reached for the paper, folded it carefully and squinted at the story. Being a septuagenarian had occasional disadvantages—one of them being the inability to see small print quite as well as when you were sixty-nine. Of course, Emma realized the difficulty was due to the poor lighting in her nephew's office.

She swung her feet off the desk, carried the paper to the reception area and stopped where the light of the late afternoon sun came through the window.

"Nancy, listen to this," she said. "The necklace containing the famous Fox Diamond was reported missing from the safe of investment counselor Benjamin Kabes on Tuesday afternoon. Mr. Kabes was taken into custody after being accused of the theft by Mrs. Genievieve Fox. . . ."

Emma was interrupted by Nancy's exasperated exclamation. The secretary's pretty face was creased into a scowl. Due to erratic surges caused by overloads on the power lines, the computer had blinked off on the last word of a ten-page report.

Nancy pulled the disk from the machine's drive, looked at Emma and smiled. "I was listening," she said, inserting a copy disk when the screen glowed again. "In fact, I put that paper on Jim's desk so he could read it. Last year, Genievieve's husband, George Fox, hired him to find an original Varga painting. Someone had broken in and stolen it from his study."

"Do you think we might get the case?" Emma asked hopefully.

Nancy shrugged. "With Jim out of town. . . ."

"Yes, it's too bad he's not here," Emma answered. There was a definite gleam in her eye.

Nancy stopped typing and gave her a level look. "Emma, what are you thinking?"

"Not a thing, dear," she said impassively.

Turning her full attention once again to the newspaper, Emma peered at the accompanying grainy photograph of a dejected, middle-aged man being put into a police car. She was certain she'd seen that face before.

"Do we have a magnifying glass?" she asked Nancy and was promptly presented with one from the desk drawer. A few minutes later, deeply engrossed in the study of the now-enlarged picture, she didn't notice the office door open.

"Hello," Nancy said. "Can I help you?"

Something in the sound of the secretary's voice made Emma straighten. The bones in the back of her neck creaked as she turned her head and saw an unhappy middle-aged man standing in the doorway. She did a double-take. It was Benjamin Kabes, the man in the photo!

"Can *we* help you?" Emma offered, quickly closing the newspaper.

"I'm looking for Jim Galveston," the man said. His otherwise amiable face was marred by a deeply furrowed brow. "I must have the wrong office."

Emma pointed at the glass doors, where large gold letters spelled: *James Galveston, Private Investigator.* "You have the right office," she told him. "But my nephew is away at a convention."

"Oh, no!" The exclamation was short and sharp. The man's slightly rounded shoulders slumped forward.

He looks defeated, Emma thought, as if the whole world just sat on him. "You're Benjamin Kabes, aren't you?" she asked. When he nodded, she said, "Jim will be gone until the end of the week."

Benjamin Kabes leaned forward and read Nancy's desk calendar upside down. "Two more days." His voice sounded very tired.

"Three really," Nancy corrected. "You have to count Saturday, too."

The weary visitor blinked, then gave the women a dispirited half-smile, and slumped into the chair in front of Nancy's desk. "What am I going to do?" he said.

Since Ben Kabes didn't seem to be expecting a reply, Emma responded with an inquiry of her own. "What do you want to do?"

His eyes flickered across the newspaper, and the half-smile was replaced by determination. "I want to hire Jim," he said. "He's an old friend. I need his help."

Before Emma could reply, Nancy interjected, "Let me try to get in touch with him, Mr. Kabes." She reached for the phone.

While Ben Kabes leaned back in the chair and watched Nancy put the call through, Emma studied his face. There was something familiar about him that she couldn't quite put her finger on. At that moment, Ben became aware of her scrutiny. He smiled, and Emma's memory clicked. During Jim's college days, a younger version of the now-infamous Ben Kabes had been one of State University's most popular male cheerleaders.

Just as Emma was about to confirm her deduction by giving him a rah-rah-rah, Nancy hung up the phone. "Jim isn't in his hotel room," she said. "But I left a message."

Ben's face sagged completely. Emma felt as though she was looking at a drowning man who had just lost a race with a shark.

"Jim will call tonight," she assured him. "When he hears about your troubles, I know he'll come home early."

Ben Kabes brightened considerably. "Do you think so?" he asked.

Emma nodded absently as another idea presented itself. With Jim away, she was the detective in charge. I was right, Emma thought. Today *is* my lucky day. Aloud, she said to Ben, "Why don't you tell us what happened?"

Ben shrugged. "It's all in the newspaper."

"That may be," Emma replied. "But they didn't print your side. And," she concluded with simple logic, "you must have one, or you wouldn't need a private investigator."

"Good point," Ben concurred. "Okay, I. . . ."

"Just a minute," Emma stopped him. "I'd like to tape what you say." She set a small recorder on the desk. "For Jim, of course," she clarified, noticing his raised eyebrow. No point in letting Ben know she'd be the one tackling his case. She pushed the record button. "You can start now."

"I didn't do it!" Ben spoke into the machine, as if answering a challenge to his honesty.

Emma liked the way he came directly to the point. Here was a man after her own heart. Before she could tell him how much she admired his straightforwardness, tears welled in his eyes.

"I *really* didn't do it," he said, directly to her this time.

She placed a protective hand on his back and patted him comfortingly, ignoring the caricature of a fretful mother hen that flitted across her mind. Jim always insisted a businesslike manner was important in crime work. Good thing he isn't here, she decided.

After Ben composed himself, she asked gently, "How did the Fox diamond get in your safe?"

"Genievieve Fox is a client of mine," Ben explained. "Or rather, her husband is. Since you've read the newspaper report, you know I'm an investment counselor. I manage George Fox's portfolio."

He paused while Emma moved the recorder closer. "Genievieve arrived at my office in a cab, with the diamond necklace. She'd gone to the bank to get it from her safe deposit box. On the way home, her car broke down. Rather than take the diamond to the garage where the car was towed, she thought of my office safe." Ben took in a large gulp of air. "Someone must have stolen the necklace when I went out to lunch. Genie was going to wear it to an awards banquet."

"Genie?" Emma asked, her mind forming a picture of small, exotic bottles and wishes come true.

"That's what everyone calls her," Ben said quickly. "She prefers it to Genievieve." He frowned. "Where was I?"

"You were returning from lunch. Please go on," Nancy said. Emma was glad to hear her friend express an interest in the case.

"Right," Ben said. "Genie was waiting. We went into my office together. I opened the safe. When I handed her the jewel box, she asked me to look at the necklace—said something was wrong with the clasp. I told her I didn't know anything about clasps, but she insisted. When she opened the lid the box was empty! She got hysterical and accused me of stealing it. She called the police. I just can't understand how Genie could think I would do such a thing." Ben winced at the memory, then asked Emma helplessly, "What possible use would I have for a diamond necklace?"

Her eyes went to his weary face. "I don't know," she said, and braced herself before asking, "Do you need money?"

He smiled grimly. "Yesterday afternoon at the police station they kept asking me that same question over and over." He leaned forward. "Would I be stupid enough to jeopardize my business and the reputation I've built up over the years?"

Emma felt sorry for him. Rhetorical questions were probably an affliction he'd acquired with shock. Benjamin Kabes hardly seemed calculating enough to be a thief. His broad face reminded her of Snoop,

A basset hound she'd once shared her home with and loved. No, she decided, neither Snoop nor Ben would steal.

Her thoughts were seconded by Nancy, who said, "The whole thing smells like a setup to me."

"Exactly what I was thinking," Emma agreed.

A relieved look crossed Ben's face. "Thank God someone believes me!"

Emma clicked off the recorder. "Nancy and I will play this for Jim when he calls. I know we can help you." As she re-wound the tape, she thought of another question. "How come the police let you go?"

"They . . . didn't, exactly," Ben confessed. He stared at his pyramided fingers. "They more or less turned their backs, and I took the opportunity to leave a little prematurely."

Emma's eyebrows nearly reached her hairline. "You mean you escaped?"

"Well . . . yes, I suppose you could say that," Ben admitted.

"Oh, Ben!" Nancy said sharply. "Don't you realize the seriousness of the charge against you?" She frowned at him.

Ben seemed to have no ready answer. Emma, recovering from the shock of his disclosure, asked, "Where will you stay? If the police are looking for you, I'm sure your home and office are under surveillance."

"I just ran. I didn't think of all the consequences," he said in a strained voice. "I only know I'm innocent, and I need Jim to prove it."

"Running away probably convinced the police of your guilt," Emma said, feeling she had to explain his predicament to him.

Ben's eyes clouded. "I guess I should turn myself in." Standing, he moved slowly toward the door. "Just knowing that Jim will be on the case gives me hope."

Once again Emma longed to comfort him. She gave into the impulse by saying, "Why don't you come to my house tonight? The invitation surprised even her, but she squared her shoulders and continued quickly, ignoring Nancy's incredulous look. "You can give yourself up after we talk to Jim."

Ben Kabes stopped twisting the doorknob and swung to face Emma. "Could I?" The hope in his voice reached his sad eyes and she could do nothing more than nod.

Nancy brought them both back to sobering reality. "The punishment for harboring a fugitive is ten years in jail."

There was silence for a long moment, then Ben said, "She's right. You could get into trouble helping me."

"Maybe," Emma said. She picked up her handbag, glanced at her watch, and walked firmly across the room. "It's after five," she said to Nancy. "And Jim doesn't pay overtime." Holding up her hand to stem their protests, she concluded decisively, "Let's go!"

"We'd better take a taxi," Nancy suggested, when they stood on the sidewalk. "I only hope we can find one in this rush hour traffic."

"Not to worry," Emma said. She stepped to the curb, put two fingers between her lips, and blew a piercing whistle. A yellow cab pulled over immediately.

Twelve minutes later, after many twists and turns, the driver dropped the trio off four blocks from where they'd started. A short walk down a quiet tree-lined street brought them to the front of a large apartment complex. "Home!" Emma declared.

"We sure took the long way," Ben commented. "No one could accuse you of not being thorough. I like the way you work," he added.

Emma accepted his praise graciously. "Thank you," she said, unlocking her front door. "In this business you can't be too careful."

She stepped aside to let Ben and Nancy enter her yellow chrome-and-glass apartment. For all its ultra-modern decor the place had a homey appearance, due in large part to the decorative needlepoint that was Emma's hobby. As she closed the door behind them, the telephone began ringing.

Emma hurried across the room to a glass end-table and touched a small walnut-colored case. The lid popped up, revealing a flat receiver.

"Hello, Aunty!" Jim's exuberant voice boomed over the wire. "I haven't been able to reach Nancy at home. Is she with you?"

"Yes, she's spending the night," Emma said. "But before I put her on, there's something important you need to know."

"What?"

Emma noticed the apprehension in his voice. "The Fox diamond has been stolen," she informed him. "Benjamin Kabes was accused of the theft. The police arrested him, but he's escaped."

"That's interesting," Jim agreed. Emma heard his sigh of relief, as if he'd expected her to tell him something much worse. "I don't think Ben Kabes is a thief," he added.

"I don't either," Emma said. "And neither does Nancy."

"Nancy? Nancy doesn't know Ben." A hint of suspicion crept back into his voice. "In fact, I don't believe you've ever met him."

"I do have a life of my own, you know," Emma reminded him. Then, relenting, she explained, "He introduced himself when he came to the office this afternoon."

"What were you doing at the office?" Jim's exasperated voice shouted in her ear before she could reply. "No! Don't tell me!"

"Okay, I won't," she retorted. "Not that it matters. Ben needed help, so Nancy and I brought him here."

"You brought him to your house?" Jim asked, spacing each word as if it were a separate question. "Aunt Emma, do you realize you're harboring a fugitive?"

"Of course, dear," Emma said promptly, though she didn't feel as confident as she tried to sound. "I'm also helping an old friend of yours."

"Don't move!" Jim commanded. "I'll be there in five minutes."

"Five minutes?" Emma repeated. "Where are you?" There was no answer. The silence stretched until she realized she was holding a dead receiver. Frustrated, she hung up and turned to face Nancy and Ben.

"That was Jim," she said, unnecessarily. "He's coming right over."

Ben frowned quizzically. "I thought he was out of town."

"The convention must have ended early," Nancy said.

"Maybe now I'll get out of this mess." Ben sounded relieved.

True to his word, Jim's tall form filled the doorway five minutes later. "Hello, Aunt Emma," he said. Leaning down, he gave his relative a quick kiss that missed her cheek.

"He's upset with me," Emma thought, noticing his formal salutation. She heaved a sigh. Would he expect her to relinquish the case? "How was the trip?" she asked. "You're back so early."

Jim's chest swelled with pride, and he ran a finger over his well-trimmed Clark Gable moustache. "The sponsors set up a mock crime. They gave us two days to find the perpetrator," he said. "I solved it in four hours. There was nothing more to do, so everyone went home."

Emma eyed her favorite nephew with mild irritation. Even as a small boy he had occasionally displayed this pompous attitude. No doubt it was something he'd inherited from his father and was totally unaware of.

Jim glanced around. "Where's Ben?" he asked. "We need to talk. Since I'm between cases, I'm sure I can help him."

"He's in the kitchen with Nancy," Emma replied. "They're cooking dinner." She hesitated over her next words, then said, "Please listen to the tape I made before you question him. That way you won't ask anything twice."

Jim gave her a lopsided grin. "If I didn't know better, I'd think you were unhappy to see me, Aunty," he chided. "Have you been 'intervening' again?"

"I didn't have enough time," Emma answered irritably.

"Don't worry. This case will probably generate lots of paperwork." Jim put his arm around her shoulders affectionately. "I'm sure Nancy won't mind if you help."

Paperwork! Emma wanted to stomp on his foot. She managed to hide her ire by loudly calling Ben into the living room. Her nephew would soon discover she had other plans!

"It's good to see you, Ben. It's been a long time," Jim said. The two men clapped each other enthusiastically on the back.

"We'll talk over dinner," Emma announced, interrupting their reunion. Taking Jim's arm, she bustled him into the dining room. "I want you to listen to the tape first," she repeated pointedly, as she showed him where to set up the recorder.

When everyone was assembled over the aromatic meat and cheese concoction Ben called "chevre burgers," Emma pressed the play button. They ate until the tape ran out and the machine clicked off, then Jim put down his fork.

"Good job, Aunty," he said, flashing her a smile. "Now, I'll proceed. There's one question you forgot to ask." He turned to Ben. "Tell me about your office safe. How many people have the combination?"

"No one but me," Ben answered. "I had the safe installed about a year ago to hold stock certificates and other important papers. Sometimes my clients leave valuables there. But I'm the only one who knows the combination. It looks bad, doesn't it?" He groaned and put his head in his hands. "I swear I didn't steal the necklace!"

Jim believed him. Emma could tell by the decisive way he picked up his water glass.

"Then we need to determine who did," he said. "How about a toast to solving this case quickly?"

●

After a morning workout, Emma entered her cheerful kitchen and found her two houseguests already making breakfast. Ben smiled a bright hello before he popped four slices of whole-wheat in the toaster. Emma blinked in surprise at the change in him. This animated countenance was far removed from the dismal form he'd presented last evening.

She looked at Nancy. "Why is he so happy?" she demanded.

"He didn't tell me," Nancy said. "But I imagine it's got something to do with Jim taking the case."

"Right," Ben said. He moved to the stove and began rescuing the poached eggs with a slotted spoon. "I've got the greatest detective in town working for me. Jimbo will prove I'm innocent. What have I got to worry about?"

"For starters," Emma reminded him, "you could worry about what you're going to do for the next week or two while Jim solves the mystery." She wiped at last night's chevre burger stain on the front of his shirt with the napkin she was holding.

"Will it take that long?" Ben asked. "I hoped he'd be able to uncover the truth today." He chewed his lip and looked down at his soiled shirt. "I have been wearing these same clothes for three. . . ."

"Nancy and I can go to your apartment and bring you a fresh outfit," Emma suggested, as if she'd just come up with the idea. She held out her hand for the keys.

"Didn't you say my place would be under surveillance?"

"A minor problem we can take care of," she assured him blithely. Nancy agreed.

●

A half hour later, Emma, holding a canvas bookbag, stepped into the cool outdoors with profound good humor. She had the keys to Ben's apartment, and she'd gotten them before Jim. The smile on her lips was jaunty, like the peacock blue combs securing her thistledown white curls.

Turning to Nancy, she asked, "Should we take a cab?" Before the young woman could comment, Emma answered her own question. "No. Exercise the body, exorcise the soul, as my aerobics instructor says."

With only a brief glance at the overcast April sky, she linked arms with Nancy and leaned into the gust of wind which threatened to sweep her from the sidewalk. Paperwork, indeed! Emma thought, as she and Nancy marched down the street. I need real work; something I can sink my teeth into.

It wasn't Emma's teeth, but Nancy's heel that sank into the soft, newly-poured cement walk in front of Ben's apartment building.

Crouched by the side of the building, Emma had an excellent view of what her creative mind, coupled with Nancy's acting ability, could make happen. As the young woman attempted to extricate her foot from the clinging, gooey mass, her shoe slipped off. With a loud cry, she stumbled against the glass door. Before she could utter a second call for help, the door swung open, and the short detective who had recently exited the police car parked at the curb caught her in his arms.

Wonderful, Emma thought. I love plans that work.

Leaving the plainclothes officer and Nancy thus entwined, she quickly entered the building through a rear exit and, within seconds, stood in front of Ben's apartment, contemplating the locked door.

"Interior" investigations always made her feel she was doing something criminal. "It's all part of the job, Aunt Emma," Jim would say, while he picked a lock. "If you want to become an expert detective like me, you'll have to get used to it."

Any lingering guilt disappeared as she remembered Ben had given her a key. Retrieving it from her pocket, she unlocked the door and, without a second glance at the well-furnished living room, hurried toward the rear of the apartment.

Ben's closet was neatly organized. Emma decided to pack his clothes before she searched for clues. She quickly pulled brown slacks, a tan jacket, and a blue striped shirt from their hangers. Advancing to the bureau, she found the rest of Ben's basic necessities lined up in military order in the top drawer. His shaving gear was in the bathroom medicine chest. When everything was secured in the bookbag, she began her search for clues.

She didn't have the slightest idea what she was looking for, but in the latest issue of *Mystery Monthly Magazine* there was an article about secret drawers in rolltop desks. And standing by the window was such a desk. Hurrying across the room, Emma opened the top. Inside was a neat stack of payment envelopes. She checked each one—utility bill, phone bill, and a charge card statement attached to a hotel receipt for Mr. and Mrs. Benjamin Kabes.

She studied the names on the hotel receipt, then glanced at the smiling face of the woman in the photograph on Ben's night table. Her musings were suddenly interrupted by voices from the outer hallway, followed by a feminine cough. Nancy's warning!

Emma detached the receipt from the statement, stuck it in her pocket, grabbed the clothes-filled bookbag and quietly opened the bedroom window. By the time the detective was back at his post, she was hurrying around the outside of the building.

●

It was midmorning when Ben, Nancy and Emma arrived on the top floor of the Galveston Building. The door was unlocked, but Jim wasn't in the office.

"He must have gone for breakfast," Nancy said. "I'll get the mail."

After the young woman left, Emma turned to Ben. "We'd better get you out of sight. You never know where the police will check next." She led him to Jim's inner sanctum.

Ben's eyes widened at the sight of the room. "Wow," he said, in awe. He walked to the huge desk and ran his hand over the gleaming mahogany top. He swiveled the leather recliner. "What a chair! Makes me want to put my feet up."

Emma chuckled. "Go ahead," she said.

Ben eased into the seat just as Emma heard Jim's voice in the outer office. She moved to the door. "I'll tell him we're here," she said over her shoulder, but the sound of annoyance in her nephew's voice made her stop. Instead of stepping into the reception area, she peeked through the crack between the door and the jamb.

". . . so . . . where have you been?" she heard Jim asking Nancy. "You know it doesn't look good when I have to answer the phone."

"I was getting the mail," Nancy answered. Her head was bent over the pile of envelopes on her desk.

Jim sighed in exasperation. "I'm talking about earlier. You weren't here to open the office this morning."

"I went with Emma to get some clothes for Ben," Nancy told him. "I think she found a clue. . . ."

"So Aunty's at it again," Jim interrupted. A self-satisfied smile played around the corners of his mouth. "Well, I'm way ahead of her. I was at Ben's office this morning and came up with some hard evidence."

"What?" Nancy asked.

Jim grinned and glanced at the gold Rolex adorning his wrist. "In due time," he said. "I've asked Genievieve Fox to stop by the office. As soon as she gets here, I'll crack this case open like a walnut. I only wish my aunt was here to see how brilliantly I've deduced the truth about the disappearing diamond."

"She's. . . ." Nancy began.

"I don't want to know where Aunty is, or what she's doing," Jim declared. "Mrs. Fox will be here any minute." He started toward his office.

In his present state of mind, Emma knew he wouldn't be glad to see her. She rushed to the desk, pulled Ben from the chair, and propelled him toward her nephew's bathroom. "Move," she commanded. "Genievieve Fox is coming. We'll hide in here."

There was barely time to arrange the door so she could see through the crack before she heard Jim's chair creak as he seated himself. After a brief silence the intercom buzzed, and Nancy's voice said, "Mrs. Fox is here."

"Send her in," Jim instructed. The chair creaked again, and Emma, peering through the crack, saw Jim stand and straighten his tie. "Hello, Mrs. Fox," he said.

"Good morning, Mr. Galveston," a husky voice answered.

"Have a seat, Mrs. Fox, and please, call me Jim."

"And you can call me Genievieve. All my friends do." The voice was heavy with feminine charm.

Emma groaned inwardly at the exchange of small talk. Get to it, Jimbo, she thought, remembering the nickname Ben had used at breakfast. But her telepathic urging had no effect on her nephew. Jim, like his aunt, hated to be rushed through his big moments.

Genievieve Fox shifted restlessly. A waft of expensive perfume

114

floated around the partly open door. Ben made a sound. Emma turned to shush him and was startled to see the dreamy look on his face as he inhaled deeply. Her attention reverted to the other room when Mrs. Fox said, "When you called, Jim, you said it was urgent."

"Yes, I did." He leaned forward. Emma recognized his "take charge" attitude, before she heard him say, "But first tell me, Genievieve, what makes you so certain Ben Kabe is a thief?"

The woman sighed in exasperation. "I handed him the box, he turned awa from me and put it in the safe. An hour later the diamond was gone." Genievieve's tone indicated irritation. "Who else had the opportunity?"

Something jiggled in Emma's mind, but refused to take a clear shape. She frowned, concentrating, while Jim continued.

"After Ben put the box in his safe, did you and he leave the office at the same time?"

"Yes," Genicvieve said. She studied her manicure. "I've been over this with the police already."

"I'm sure you have," Jim said, "but bear with me." His rich baritone was soothing.

"Ben walks to the Duck and Wing Cafe every day for lunch," Genievieve said. "He orders the special of the day and stays at the cafe from twelve to one. . . ."

"How come she knows so much about your habits?" Emma whispered to Ben. Before he could answer, the thing that had been bothering her jelled. She forgot she and Ben were supposed to be hiding. Pulling the bathroom door open, she marched out to confront Genievieve Fox.

"What is going on?" Jim demanded. "Nancy!" he yelled. Emma saw his face redden under his sun-lamp tan, but she ignored his pique.

"That's been the problem all along," she exclaimed as Nancy rushed through the door. "Not only does she know a lot about Ben, but Ben knows quite a bit about—Genie."

"Who?" Jim asked.

"Genie," Emma reiterated patiently. "A lover's pet name for Genievieve."

"Of course," Nancy said.

Ben stepped from the bathroom. "Genie and I are not lovers," he stated firmly.

Genievieve Fox, who hadn't said anything since Emma burst into the room, jumped to her feet at the sight of Ben and blurted, "What are you doing here?"

Jim rapped his pencil on the desk impatiently. "Aunt Emma," he said sternly.

"Emma smiled at him. "Don't you see? The jewel box gave it away."

"What?" Jim's tone demanded an answer.

"The box that held the necklace," Emma clarified. "I kept wondering why the thief removed the necklace, then returned the empty box to the safe. Why not just steal the whole thing?"

"Ben didn't think I'd open the box until I got home," Genievieve interrupted. She glared at the investment counselor. Ben moved closer to Jim.

"Then why did you insist on showing him the necklace?" Emma asked.

The color drained from Genievieve's carefully made-up face. "I don't have to answer your questions," she snapped. Gathering her handbag, she turned to leave. Nancy blocked the door.

"The diamond was never in the box, was it, Mrs. Fox?" Emma asked, pressing her attack.

"What a ridiculous remark!" Genievieve answered in a taut voice.

Jim pursed his lips. "My aunt's theory makes sense," he observed. "It's very close to mine. Except. . . . he paused, and gave Emma a less-than-confident look. "Why should she want to frame Ben?"

"Because she must have seen this in his office before he took it home!" Emma pulled the hotel receipt from her pocket, showed it to Genievieve, then handed it to Jim.

"'Hell hath no fury,'" Nancy quoted.

Genievieve stared at the secretary for a moment, than sank into the chair. "You're right," she said, in a defeated voice. "I was in Ben's office last week. I went there to tell him I'd finally decided to leave my husband."

"I didn't think you'd ever leave George for me." Ben sounded as though he couldn't believe what he'd just heard.

"It's all I thought about until I saw that . . . that Mr. and Mrs. Benjamin Kabes thing lying on your desk." Her tear-filled eyes narrowed angrily. "How could you?"

"Genie," he said sadly, "I wish I knew what you were talking about. We agreed not to see each other while you were married, but you know I love you."

"You certainly have a funny way of showing it." The sophisticated woman's voice shook as she said the words.

Emma could tell from Ben's blank expression that he was totally perplexed. Always the matchmaker, she hurried to explain. "It's a little complicated. . . ."

Jim stood. "Aunt Emma, pleeaase," he admonished. "Before you jumped out of the bathroom and messed up this whole case it was simple and obvious. . . ."

"Sit down, dear," Emma told him. She waited until he did before she continued. "The only thing obvious is that a man and a woman spent the night in a hotel room under the name Mr. and Mrs. Benjamin Kabes. However, I noticed the address on the receipt was not Ben's. Since Ben is single, why would he bother using a false address? So, two hours ago, while you were checking his office, I let my fingers solve the mystery."

When everyone was looking at her expectantly, Emma paused. She was truly savoring the moment, until Jim demanded, "Aunt Emma! Can we get on with this?"

Poor dear, she thought. I'd better be gentle. She smiled at him. "You couldn't have known, Jim, because you didn't have the clue I did. The address on the hotel receipt matched the one in the phone book for Mr. and Mrs. Benjamin Kabes, Senior—Ben's mother and father. Last week they spent an evening visiting him and decided it was too late to drive home."

"That doesn't explain the clue I found," Jim's chiseled lips tightened in mulish stubbornness.

"What clue?" Nancy asked. "You never did tell us."

"Two tickets to Mexico. Which indicates. . . ."

"They're for my parents' fortieth wedding anniversary," Ben spoke up. "I wanted to surprise them with a cruise."

"Right! Ties in with my theory exactly," Jim agreed. Emma stared in amazement as he continued without a pause. "I knew Ben wasn't a thief."

"And I should have known he'd never be unfaithful to the woman he loves," Genievieve said, her steamy eyes focused on her beloved's smiling face. "Oh, Benji, can you ever forgive me?"

After Jim promised to talk to his friends on the police force and explain that Genievieve had mistakenly given Ben an empty box, the wealthy woman and the investment counselor left the office, arms entwined.

Jim settled into his chair, seesawed into position, and set his feet on the gleaming mahogany desk. "Another case well solved," he said in satisfaction.

"Yes," Emma agreed. She winked at Nancy. "And after lunch, you can type up the paperwork. Okay, Jimbo?"

Hot as a Pistol

KAREN WILSON

*T*he ringing phone saved me from the clutches of humidity-induced catatonia. The voice on the other end rescued me from the tedium of scaring up another counterfeit jeans case. As the ceiling fan in the outer office turned hopelessly, my young detecting career moved beyond the bread-and-butter stage. I had my first real caper, as Uncle Raymond would have said.

Beverly Grayson gave me the particulars with just a touch of panic in her voice. Wanda James, her business partner, had missed an appointment a few hours earlier and her house seemed "funny." Ransacked? No. Forced entry? No. Just funny, like what's wrong with this picture. Could she prevail upon my professional expertise for advice on what to do next?

I had a serious case of the curiosities for Beverly and she knew it. We had met for drinks a few times and had worked all the way up to overt flirtation. Beverly had an anachronistic air about her, one that said "good breeding." She held herself tall and straight, creating the illusion of modelesque dimensions. In reality, she stood a shade under five feet, six inches and was much too well-endowed for the current fashions. Her blond hair grew thick and just beyond her shoulders. She pushed it back from her face frequently with a slender, manicured hand. Beverly's blue eyes changed from sparkling to smoldering to stone-cold, depending on her mood. I preferred the smoldering mood myself. Then, her demeanor softened and the promise of her full lips was unmistakable.

Beverly had introduced me to Wanda on our second Happy Hour date. The bar happened to be close to their casting agency, and Wanda happened to drop by after working a little later than everyone else. Wanda, a few years older than Beverly, was quick with a smile. As aloof as Beverly seemed, Wanda came off as your best friend for years now. The way she looked me up and down and over without missing a beat in the conversation also told me Wanda was a friendly woman, very friendly.

As soon as Beverly mentioned that I was a detective—"a female Magnum" is how she put it—Wanda launched into a long story about mysterious phone calls at three a.m., shadows around her house, and a spine-tingling close call on the canyon roads. And the punch line was that she, Wanda, had been on the receiving end of these spookies for a couple of weeks now.

Who was behind it all? She didn't know. Who did she think was behind it? She couldn't imagine. Had she called the police? Once; they said they'd rather wait to get involved. Wait? Until something happened. Did she feel like something was going to happen? Maybe. Did she want a private investigator? Maybe, she'd call me. I gave Wanda my card and Beverly gave me a smile.

A week later, Beverly hired me to find Wanda James.

The Civic Center high that day was ninety-eight and the humidity stayed around eighty percent. What had happened to Southern California's perfect weather? Why live in L.A. when it feels like New York without the museums? Had Beverly sounded too upset to be interested in dinner? Just what were the ethics of personal involvements with clients? I couldn't remember Sam Spade passing up the company of a beautiful woman just because he worked for her. And none of Uncle Raymond's old pals had mentioned any special restrictions for lesbian detectives. Precedent was on my side.

Driving west on Melrose, then Sunset into the afternoon sun, I let my heat-dulled brain wander about those sundry tracks. How to turn drinks into dinner and dinner into a weekend away constituted the most consistent train of thought I had on the way to meet with Beverly at Wanda's Laurel Canyon home.

About twenty minutes after her call, I parked the loaner car I'd been using for a week in the driveway of a square Spanish-style stucco abode.

The house, with its red tile roof, sat flush against the canyon wall in the Hollywood Hills. And Beverly's white Mercedes sat in the carport, top down. I could just see her driving up the Coast Highway at sunset, blond hair swept back in the wind, too cool. I put on my linen jacket and felt too hot.

"Nice hat." Beverly complimented my broad-brim straw number as she let me in.

She calmly offered me a cold drink and led the way to a canvas-covered deck on the north side of the house.

"The air conditioning seems to have been off for hours," she explained. "It's actually cooler out here since the house was all closed up."

We sat in cushioned wicker chairs, sipping gin and tonic, evoking images of memsahibs waiting for the cricket match to resume. It could have been our white ensembles—hers of silk—which put me in mind of colonial India. I continued to lose the here-and-now as Beverly's thick blonde hair fell across her left eye when she moved to set her drink on the table between us. Suddenly, I was transported to a Veronica Lake movie. Did that make me Alan Ladd? The fact that he was a bad guy in that movie and I'm hardly ever a bad guy got me back to the present. That and Beverly's questions.

"Do you think I should be worried? What do you think could have happened to her? Did you believe that story of hers, you know, about someone calling and threatening her?" Beverly rushed her words despite an obvious effort to sound in charge.

"Don't worry until there's some reason. That's my motto," I reassured her.

"It's just not like her to not show up. And her car's gone. So she went *somewhere*." Beads of perspiration covered her upper lip

"Any place she likes to go to get away, to relax?" Time to get to work.

"No. Ever since we've been—since I've known Wanda, she's never wanted to go away, never taken a vacation."

"Sounds like a hard-working partner."

"She is, very."

"And what kind of lover?"

Beverly looked at me, staring hard into my eyes.

"Good," she said, finally, her eyes darting from mine to her drink.

"Most of the time." She took a long drink then looked back at me. There was some fresh pain in those blue eyes.

"If you've finished your drink, we should look inside for clues," she commanded politely.

I winced at the word "clues." Since I rarely recognized a clue as such until it smacked me in the face, I hated being watched while I searched for the little buggers. Couldn't get out of it this time, though.

I followed Beverly back inside and through the house. Her familiarity told me it had been their home, hers and Wanda's. The furnishings were California contemporary—lots of casual fabrics, restful colors, natural woods, hints of the sea, suggestions of the desert. They seemed like Beverly's ideas. The Wanda touches were film scripts stacked and strewn around the living room with copies of the *Hollywood Reporter* thrown in for color.

"Wanda's the reader," Beverly explained. "I'm the people-watcher."

And the one to watch, I thought, admiringly.

The kitchen had an abandoned look. As I opened cupboards, one after another, to find emptiness, Beverly confirmed my suspicion.

"Cooking never held much fascination for Wanda, so I took all the kitchen equipment when I left."

"Did she ever ask what this room was for?"

Beverly smiled and I sighed inside. Lovely, that smile.

The bedroom looked comfortable and thoroughly understood. It contained, barely, a brass bed, high and wide and gleaming. Four oversized pillows stood up against the headboard, each one with a different colored case. The bed coverings were neatly in place and a pair of dark blue cotton pajamas lay folded at the end of the bed.

I noticed something missing from one wall.

"What was here?" I asked, pointing out the dingy wall surrounding a clean patch.

Beverly looked stunned and took a moment to answer.

"My portrait," she said quietly. "I guess she didn't want to look at me anymore."

"Is anything else missing? Look around," I prompted.

Beverly went through the closet while I surveyed the top of the nightstand next to the bed. It held the standard fare—a lamp, a clock radio, and some paperbacks. Detective novels, three of them, with stiff covers and broken spines. Recently purchased, recently read.

"Her overnight bag is gone, but I can't be sure about the clothes," Beverly reported.

We went through the house once more, looking for anything unusual. The clues weren't jumping up to introduce themselves. The bathroom appeared freshly cleaned, but the smell of Lysol didn't inspire any startling realizations. The few plants around were healthy, though suffering from the heat. The same could be said for Beverly and me. We met again in the bedroom.

"You mentioned on the phone that she missed a meeting. Where and what time?" I asked as Beverly sat down on the bed.

"Two o'clock at Tommy Tang's."

I had passed the trendy West Hollywood eatery on my way there.

"When was the appointment set up?" I leaned against the wall where the portrait had been.

"Yesterday."

"Who were you meeting?"

"An agent who has been all over us to cast 'the next James Dean.'"

"Isn't it difficult to work with an ex?"

"Sometimes. But we could hardly avoid each other in such a small community, now could we?"

I had to agree with her. The social avenues used by most lesbians virtually guaranteed run-ins to former lovers, even in L.A.

"So, you get along? Still friends?" I pressed.

"Yes, still good friends."

"Why did you break up?"

Beverly trained ice-cold blue eyes on me again.

"I don't see that that is any of your business," she said.

If "why" was a button, "when" probably was, too. I backed off the personal stuff.

"Maybe she had another appointment."

"No, I checked with Ronald, her secretary. Her schedule was clear," she said calmly.

"Have you asked the police to find Wanda?"

"I called them. They won't accept a missing person report for twenty-four hours. They weren't convinced that something has happened to her."

"What makes you think something has?"

Beverly slumped back against the brass headboard and covered her face with her hands.

"She told you about the phone calls, the car that tried to run her off the road. She's been seeing someone she shouldn't be seeing. Maybe a married woman. Men are not very understanding about their wives sleeping with other women, as I'm sure you know." She looked up and smiled wanly.

"Not first-hand." I didn't smile back. "What's this woman's name?"

"I don't know. I really don't know anything except that Wanda has been uptight for weeks now." She sat up straight.

"Is this woman the reason you split up?" I sat down on the bed next to her.

She looked away and blinked quickly several times.

"I couldn't believe it when I found out." She faced me, clear-eyed. "After all we had been to each other—friends, lovers, partners. Her arrogance was unbelievable!"

"So why are you so concerned about her now?"

"She's still my friend, despite all that has happened. And she is my business partner, after all. I must do the right thing by her, don't you agree?" She knitted her brow in a serious manner.

"Sure. But I'll need more to go on that just a maybe married woman and her cuckolded husband."

"Just tell me what you want."

She was in my arms before I could say "Mary Astor." Her hot slender fingers caressed the back of my neck. I felt flushed, the blood pounding in my head, as Beverly pulled me toward her. That kiss sealed my fate.

●

I left Wanda's house an hour later with a list of her friends, a check for two hundred dollars, and a little confusion over whether I had taken advantage of Beverly or she had taken advantage of me. It didn't really matter; we both had enjoyed ourselves, heat and all.

At the end of the street, I pulled into a driveway and waited for Beverly to go past. The white Mercedes zipped by about five minutes later. With the coast clear, I returned to Wanda's.

Parking in the carport, I noticed a large rug covering something square at the rear of the structure. When I lifted the rug, I was face-to-face with a life-sized image of Beverly Grayson, wearing nothing but a Panama hat. I stepped back to take in the full effect of the painting. Beverly sat cross-legged on a large lush pillow decorated with a tropical print. Her hair, past waist-length, was strategically arranged so that it barely covered her breasts, tantalizing the beholder of the scene. Her smile of slight amusement was designed to launch magnificent rumors about its source. I put the rug back over the framed canvas. The effect of the painting was almost as overwhelming as Beverly herself. I understood why Wanda had taken it down.

Back on the job, I jimmied the lock on the side door, just like Uncle Raymond had taught me, and went inside. I went back to the bedroom to check out the closet for myself this time. The clothes rack didn't give up anything, but the shoe rack on the floor did. Three pairs of prongs were empty.

A personal phone directory next to the telephone in the living room had caught my eye earlier. When I opened it, a list of speed-dial codes and numbers sat on the top. Naturally, I filched the list. Beverly had given me the names of three people—Kellie Banks, Betty Smith, and Ronald Thomas, Wanda's secretary. Who had only three friends? Wanda's speed-dial list had Ronald's number on the top line followed by a dozen others. The name Emily MacNeil and a local phone number was penciled in at the very top of the page. Betty Smith wasn't on the list. I dialed the number Beverly had written down next to the name. The man who answered said no one named Smith lived there.

Kellie Banks, the name under Ronald's on Wanda's list, had a West Hollywood exchange, indicating that she probably lived just to the south, so I gave her a call next.

According to Ms. Banks, she hadn't seen Wanda James for at least three weeks and she didn't care if she never saw her again. Seems that Wanda had made a pass at Kellie's girlfriend at a Memorial Day barbecue. If Wanda had disappeared, Kellie thought it likely that she'd run off with somebody else's partner.

I learned that much on the phone. When I asked to stop by, Kellie agreed immediately. Wanda and Beverly, apparently, was an irresistible subject for discussion.

A short time later I stood on the front porch of Kellie's small duplex. Once inside, I took an iced tea and another scathing earful about Wanda from the middle-aged woman. Kellie's paintings covered her living room walls, while an easel was propped open in the dining room, which also served as an art studio.

"Does Wanda make a habit of chasing other women's lovers?" I asked once we sat down.

"Wanda makes a habit of chasing women," Kellie answered with a firm nod of her smallish head. A dollop of gray paint clumped a few strands of her black hair together just above her right eyebrow.

"So, she and Beverly had an open relationship?" I ventured.

Beverly sent you here, right?" I nodded. "You don't know her, though, do you?" I shook my head, no. "Beverly is loyal to a fault. And Wanda is that fault. She forgave Wanda time and again, believing her when she said she'd never do it again. Until this last time."

"You mean the married woman?" I asked.

"I don't know if she was married or not. But, whoever it was, it was the last straw for Beverly. She moved out and told Wanda their relationship was strictly business from now on."

"How long ago was that?"

"A couple of months or so."

"What do you think made Beverly change?"

I heard that Wanda brazenly brought her paramour-of-the-month to an office party. Beverly was mortified."

"But you don't have any idea who that was?"

"Who could keep up with Wanda's women?" Kellie laughed.

I thanked her for the cold drink and her time.

As Kellie walked me to the door, I asked how she had come to know Wanda and Beverly.

"Beverly commissioned me to paint her portrait about a year ago. It was a birthday present. Wanda loved it, just loved it. But all the while Beverly was sitting for me, I had the distinct impression she was really having the portrait done for herself. I was surprised to hear she didn't take it with her when she moved out."

"Wanda has taken it down now," I told Kellie.

"Probably too hard to look at what she can't have anymore."

I took my leave and thanked my lucky stars once again that people love to talk about their friends.

Since I was near home, I stopped off to shower and change clothes. As I unlocked the door, the stale, hot, smog-tinged air hit me like exhaust from a bus on a tour of the stars' homes. The first order of business, I decided, was to turn on the box fan. I dropped the mail on the kitchen table and checked with my answering service. Jane gave me two messages—one from my last client, insisting that the check was in the mail, and one from Gayle, my mechanic, saying the Riley was running like clockwork once again. Jane wished me a cool night and gave me the impression she would have accepted an offer for a hot one. But the humidity was too high, and I had work to do.

I showered and found another set of whites for the evening. A black, loosely-knotted tie added some contrast and a summer-weight fedora, also black, added some class.

With picking up the Riley, rustling up some dinner, and trying to find Wanda James all vying to be next on the agenda, I called Ronald Thomas, Wanda's secretary. Sure, he said, I could come over, providing I made it quick. Sounded like a busy chap.

Before leaving, I tried calling the penciled-in name on Wanda's phone list, Emily MacNeil, but there was no answer. Another time, Emily.

The short drive to Santa Monica Boulevard and the garage was pleasant enough in eighty-five degrees. Friday night brought out all the neighborhood variety. Two grandmothers, round and soft, sat on the sidewalk in kitchen chairs, swapping complaints about the snores of old men. Dark-haired olive-skinned boys pedaled black bicycles in and out of the street. Their little sisters squealed through a game of tag. As I got closer to the Boulevard, the children gave way to adolescents, fashion victims and rock 'n roll casualties, and no-deposit, no-return runaways. Home sweet home. The boys, the girls, the men about to coming, the women about to work—the street had room for them all. And me, too.

The Riley kicked over perfectly. I put the top down. It's going to be a fine night, I thought, as I slid behind the wheel and waved a quick goodbye to Gayle. It's always a fine night when I'm working and the Riley's working at the same time.

Ronald lived in Silver Lake, so I took Santa Monica to Sunset

Boulevard and the heart of the district. Along the way, the royal blue Riley attracted its usual number of admiring looks and "what is it?" questions. It had been Uncle Raymond's pride and joy, and I knew why every time I drove the British sportster. The large fenders, the remnant of a running board, the front grillwork, the leather seats, all gave me a rush of the 'forties. Boplicity!

●

"You must be Wiggins, right?" Ronald answered the door.

"Yes." I extended my hand, which he took for a second.

"Come in, come in." He stepped back and waved me in. "I have to finish dressing, but we can talk. Sit, sit."

I sat down as Ronald, tall, thin, and slightly balding, padded away in bare feet. He returned a minute later with some socks and western boots. He sat across from me on a leather couch.

"So, on the phone you said something about Wanda?" He started putting on the socks.

"Right. She's apparently missing, and Beverly has hired me to find her."

"No, she's not."

"She's not what?"

"Missing."

"How do you know?"

"Because she told me she was going to her beach house this weekend."

"And you didn't tell Beverly?"

"Wanda told me not to. She said Beverly would be better off if she didn't know about her plans."

"Did those plans involve a married woman?"

"Not *very* married, if she can get away for the weekend, wouldn't you say?"

"Beverly mentioned Wanda had an appointment with an agent. Know anything about it?

"Sure. Beverly told me to remind Wanda about it, so I called Wanda in Malibu this morning." Ronald left the room again.

"This morning?" I called after him. There was no answer until he returned, putting a leather vest on over his white western shirt.

"What?"

"You talked to Wanda *this* morning?"

"Actually, I talked to Emily. She said Wanda was cooling off or something." He looked at himself approvingly in a full-length mirror on the back of the front door.

"What did she mean?"

"They had just had an argument, you know, a lovers' quarrel."

"Is Emily's last name MacNeil?"

"Yep." Ronald took a pair of spurs off a hat rack on the wall and sat down again.

"And Beverly didn't know anything about Wanda's being at her beach house?"

"Nope. It was just our little secret. Are you going to tell her?" He put the spurs on the boots.

"She hired me to find Wanda. Wanda didn't hire me not to."

"If you tell her, it's my ass, I'm sure." Ronald stood up and walked around the room, listening to the spurs jingle-jangle. "Beverly'll probably get hysterical again."

"You don't see too many people wearing spurs in L.A. anymore," I said as I stood up.

"You just don't go to the right places, Wiggins."

"Don't they get a little dangerous on the dance floor?"

"Only if you move your feet." He winked.

The doorbell rang and Ronald's date arrived. I had one more question for Ronald.

"Why would Beverly get hysterical about Wanda's weekend plans?"

"Because, up until about three weeks ago, Beverly and Emily were The Hot Twosome around town."

I wished the cowboys happy trails and headed for the nearest pay phone.

One number on Wanda's list had the word "beach" next to it. I dropped in my twenty cents and marveled at my knack for finding missing people. A busy signal rewarded my cleverness. I waited a few minutes and tried the number again. Still busy. I tried another number.

Beverly answered immediately after the first ring.

"I think I've located Wanda."

"So soon?"

"You're paying me to be efficient. I need your help to make sure she's okay."

"I'm also paying you to be effective, darling. What kind of help could you possibly need from me?"

"I think Wanda's at her beach house."

"So you're going to Malibu?"

"Why not drive out there together? You know where it is, right?"

"You go, sweetheart. This afternoon has left me exhausted."

Her tone puzzled and stroked me at the same time. I gambled for some clarity.

"She may be with Emily MacNeil." I tossed out the name for effect.

"So she's seeing that precious little bird again," Beverly said archly. "I'm not surprised. Well, tell Wanda she'd better have another excuse for missing the meeting today."

Obviously, the boss had no intention of going to Malibu with me, so I wrote down the directions to the beach house and said I'd call her from there.

"Thanks so much, darling. I don't know what I would have done without you," Beverly purred across the telephone line.

I found myself saying, "Don't worry, honey, I'll take care of everything" and wondering what the hell I meant.

I went to Canter's for some dinner and some time. Loretta, the waitress, gave me both with a smile and no chitchat.

Beverly had seemed so concerned about Wanda this afternoon. On the phone, though, she sounded indifferent to news of Wanda. The more I thought about her story, the more holes I saw. A warning bell was sounding. Beautiful women are a dangerous weakness in any line of work. And most of the time I didn't even try to resist their charms. Beverly had plenty not to resist. But just how many times had I been seduced so far on this case? Where was Wanda James? Did it matter? And Emily MacNeil was beginning to sound like the stuff dreams are made of. Or nightmares.

●

The beach house was located in the far north end of Malibu, where the rich not only had the sand and the surf, but the space to enjoy them. My puzzlement over Beverly was pushed aside as I got closer and closer to the house. By the time I pulled into the driveway of Wanda's hideaway and got out of the Riley, I had my old spring back. My heart had back its old song. Life was good, it was cool.

I knocked on the door. The door opened slightly from the pressure of my knock. I pushed it back slowly. The pulsating sound of a telephone left off the hook too long came from somewhere inside.

Moonlight flooded the dark room, revealing the standard living room arrangement of couch framed by chairs and end tables. I saw something long and lumpy on the couch. Five cautious steps and I was staring at a nude woman I had never seen before. Laid out, she was, waiting for a dirge to begin.

●

Blue ocean, cool breezes, moonlight shimmering, Beverly dancing slowly, closer, closer. The moonlight makes an aura around her, silky white, swaying closer, closer. Hair flying gently and hands touching softly, cool skin on cool skin. Warm lips brush, tingling, the blue starts to turn green, moonlight bleaches to sunlight. Closer, closer, Beverly caressing, covering. Flesh on flesh, steaming in the too-bright whiteness. Circles, pools of sweat engulf the tropical bed. Drenching, drained, soaking wet, stone dead.

I came to. Lying next to a couch on a scratchy carpet with an even worse headache than I had brought from L.A., I had the overwhelming desire to be someplace else. Anyplace else.

A lamp on a table at the far end of the couch had been turned on since my entrance. I sat up slowly, leaning upright against the chair nearest the door. The woman I had seen just before hitting the floor was still lying on the couch. A blanket had been spread over her body since my last glimpse. Rubbing the place where the throbbing was the worst, I discovered a tender bump at the base of my skull. The room was still and much too quiet.

I stood up to take a closer look at the body. The room started spinning. I sat down and contemplated my silent companion. She looked to be in her late twenties, a little on the frail side. There was blood on the side of her mouth and bruises on her neck. Her face had a repose to it that suggested peaceful slumber. Once the nauseous feeling subsided, I reached over toward her wrist and checked for a pulse. The coldness of the flesh told me it was a waste of time. She had been dead for a spell, maybe hours.

A tiny stream of sweat ran down my back. Murder was not what I was looking for. A little romance, a little excitement, maybe a car chase here and there, but not the big M. "Alibi" suddenly had new meaning in my life.

"Forget something? Or do you just want to make sure you've done the job right?" Wanda's voice boomed at me from behind.

I whirled to face her and found a gun directed at the general vicinity of my heart.

"I came looking for you," I told her, fighting back the nausea that threatened to overtake me.

"That's a likely story. Why? Am I missing or something?"

Her jaw was set firmly and her lips pursed intently. Big-boned and muscular, her body was taut, yet tentative as she stood in the middle of the room. A well-timed "boo" would have sent her ten feet in the air. The dampness of her Hawaiian shirt suggested that Wanda had been sweating it out for a while.

"Beverly thought you were. She hired me to find you."

"Oh, I'm sure she put you up to all of this. How long have you two been planning this?"

"Planning what?" I asked innocently.

"You're good at playing dumb, Wiggins. *If* you're playing."

I winced. Sticks and stones. . . .

"Wanda, I really don't know what you're talking about."

"Which one of you actually killed Emily?"

Wanda's unsteady pistol hand betrayed the serious coldness in her eyes. I tried to think of a way to put some distance between myself and this obviously distraught woman. But I was faced with an uncharacteristic lack of inspiration.

"Listen, Wanda, that nighty-night rap you gave me has made it hard to be as sharp as I would like during a conversation where my life hangs in the balance. Do you think I could have some ice and a towel?"

"Help yourself. The kitchen's that way."

Wanda motioned toward the far end of the living room. She followed me closely as I headed toward the slight relief of a cold compress.

I leaned against the sink as Wanda stood in the doorway, blocking the only obvious escape route. As if I were capable of moving that fast.

"So, how much are you getting for this?" Wanda jerked her head toward the living room.

"You're not in a position to be pinning raps," I said. "After all, it's your house, your girlfriend, your ex-girlfriend's ex. And you and Emily had a fight just this morning, didn't you? Could be jealous rage reared its ugly head."

"You're a real smart-ass, aren't you, Wiggins?" Wanda began to seethe. "Oh, yes, jealous rage is right. You and Beverly are perfect for each other. Two of the high and mighty ones. You both think you can get by on your good looks and everybody else's hard work. Beverly used me and she's using you. She even tried to use Emily." Wanda's voice trailed off as she let out a long cracked breath. "Emily and I argued over when I should leave the agency. She thought I should give Beverly more notice."

I wiped my face with the compress and got a whiff of familiar perfume. I took another hit. Having a keen sense of smell always had been a blessing, but never handier than on this job. The perfume was unmistakably Beverly's.

The picture was getting fuzzier and it had nothing to do with my concussion. My gut said Wanda didn't kill Emily. My ego wouldn't let me believe that Beverly had and then set me up to take the fall.

"Did you have a business appointment scheduled today?" I asked.

"Yeah, Beverly arranged it." Tears stained Wanda's cheeks.

"Where?"

"Newport Beach. I was two hours down there and two hours back on the damned freeway for nothing."

"What do you mean?"

"The guy with 'the next James Dean' never showed."

"When did you get back here?"

"Right before you came in. I hadn't even put on the lights."

It took some smooth talking, but I convinced Wanda that we needed Beverly to find out what happened to Emily, and Beverly wasn't about to come to Malibu. I suggested Wanda call the police and bring them to my office in an hour. She listened as I phoned Beverly and told her to meet me there, too. Beverly balked at first. But when I mentioned I might need an alibi, she found a reason to be there. I left Wanda sitting quietly beside Emily's body.

The trip back saw my headache increase ever so much and my confusion diminish ever so slightly. I turned off the Pacific Coast Highway at Sunset and headed for West Hollywood, anxious to put some questions to Beverly before the coppers arrived.

The streets of the city were far from deserted that time of the night, but the deep shadows made the desperate side of urban life more evident. I startled a prostitute and her customer negotiating in the doorway of the Somner Building when I walked up. We all apologized for being there.

Up on the fourth floor, I unlocked the outer office door with no sign of Beverly. My shirt stuck to me like used gum. The building was a swelter box at night, without air conditioning. Flipping on the lights to both offices, I crossed to the inner office and began opening windows.

As I reached the last window, Beverly walked in, dressed in an aquamarine jumpsuit that did everything for her eyes. The still-fresh image of young Emily MacNeil kept me from being more than momentarily distracted.

"You sounded so serious on the phone, darling. Is anything wrong?" Beverly asked as she entered the office.

"I'm afraid so. I have some bad news for you, sweetheart," I said.

"You know, I'm very glad to see you," Beverly moved closer to me.

You may not be in a few minutes, I thought, stepping away from her and toward the liquor cabinet.

"Can I get you a drink?" I asked.

"I'll take Scotch, if you have it, with a little water," she said, smiling.

I fixed Beverly's drink and a gin and tonic for myself, while Beverly sat stiffly on the worn couch. I felt the gulf between us grow. The stone-coldness behind the smoldering blue eyes was glinting through.

"I didn't find Wanda," I told her as I handed her the drink.

"You said she was at the beach house."

"I said I *thought* she was at the beach house. I did find a woman there. But she couldn't tell me anything about Wanda."

Beverly took a drink before she asked, "Why not?"

"Because she was dead."

"How awful! What happened?"

"It looks like murder."

"Do you think Wanda killed her?"

"It's possible. It may explain why Wanda disappeared. Anyway, I thought you might want to call a lawyer before I call the police."

"Me? Why should I call a lawyer?"

"For Wanda."

"Oh, of course."

"In the meantime, I'll keep looking for her," I said as I finished my drink. "And her current flame."

"I thought you said you found Emily at the beach house."

"I found a murdered young woman. I don't know who she was."

I took a long drink as Beverly tried to avoid reacting to her slip.

"Tell me about your break-up with Wanda," I said.

"It was over Emily, of course," she asserted coolly. "Wanda was cheating on me and I wouldn't stand for it."

"It wasn't the first time Wanda had cheated on you."

She took in the statement with no visible reaction.

"I mean, Wanda sort of made a habit of cheating, didn't she?" I pressed.

"She's easily flattered. We run into a lot of young actresses, eager to get into the movies, and, well, Wanda allows their flirtations to go to her head."

"But what made Emily MacNeil different? Why split up over one more pretty face?"

"Wanda was making a fool of me in public," Beverly said matter-of-factly. "Emily was making a fool of Wanda, encouraging her to give up the agency and become a screenwriter, of all things!"

"Did you hire me to take the rap for you or for Wanda?"

A knock on the door froze Beverly's look of surprise.

"That'll be Wanda," I said as I left the room.

By the time I let Wanda in and we returned to the inner office, Beverly had recovered her familiar poise and was standing behind my desk. Wanda and I stopped dead in our tracks at the sight of my gun in Beverly's steady hand.

"Move over there." Beverly motioned toward the couch with the pistol. "Both of you."

Wanda edged out of her line of fire.

"That gun's not loaded, Beverly," I said. "I just keep it around to show clients who think detectives should pack hardware."

Beverly looked at me then looked at the gun. She aimed at Wanda's chest and pulled the trigger. Twice. She pointed the .38 at me for the third try. How did I get so lucky as to be with not one, but two women who would have killed me? I took the useless weapon from Beverly as she staggered wearily to the couch.

"The police are on the way," Wanda said as I put the gun back in the top desk drawer.

Beverly stood up and made a dash for the door. Catching her arm, Wanda slammed the door and locked it before she could escape.

"You're not going anywhere!" Wanda spat at her as she shoved Beverly in my direction.

I caught her before she could fall against the desk. When I looked into her stone-cold blue eyes, the Beverly I had felt close to a few hours before wasn't there.

"Let me go," she pleaded. "I'll give you five thousand dollars."

I raised my eyebrows.

"Ten thousand," she offered.

"How about the truth?" I counter-offered.

"The truth?" She wheeled out of my grasp to face the door Wanda stood blocking. "You mean the truth about Wanda's ingratitude and disloyalty?

"Who gave you your start, Wanda?" Beverly hissed. "Who taught you how to land the big contracts? Who made sure you could afford that Ferrari? How many times did I take you back, Wanda? And what have you done for me? You cheated, you lied, and then you let this parasite Emily make a shambles of the best agency in the business!"

"She was good for me, Beverly. I know you tried to seduce her, tried to poison her against me. But you and I were through and nothing was going to change that."

"Who are you to decide we were through? No one leaves me! I leave them!" Beverly screamed at Wanda.

"You left Emily dead!" Wanda screamed back.

"Liar!" Beverly ignored Wanda and turned toward me. "Don't you see I could never kill anyone? You found Emily dead in Wanda's house. Wanda obviously has a vile temper and no scruples. Let's turn her over to the police and get out of here. We can go anywhere you want." The smoldering look came back into her eyes. I was getting pretty heated myself.

"But, angel, what makes you think you can get away with it?" I asked. The perspiration beaded on her upper lip.

"With your help, the police will believe me. I called you because I was concerned for my missing friend, remember? And everyone knows I liked Emily enormously. Why would I harm her?"

"Why, indeed? Could it be you'd met your match? Not only was Emily taking your woman, but threatening your livelihood and resisting your charms as well. So, you sent Wanda on a wild goose chase to Newport Beach, strangled the young lady, and called me for a cover. Not a bad day's work."

"You're too smart for your own good, Wiggins."

"No," Wanda said. "Too smart for *your* own good."

Another knock on the outer door told us that the Los Angeles county sheriff's deputies had arrived. Beverly took my arm as Wanda went to let them in.

"Please, you don't want to do this. You can't do this to me. Whatever you want, just tell me. We're a good team. I thought you wanted me. . . ."

Her smoldering eyes were there, but all I could think about was the cold clammy wrist of Emily MacNeil.

"I depended on you, just like I depended on Wanda. All I get is betrayal. It's just not fair," Beverly lamented as a female deputy escorted her from the office.

Wanda and I followed the squad car to the sheriff's station to give our statements.

I left the station just as dawn broke. Beverly had had it all—looks, money, success. But looks, money and success aren't everything, as my granny used to say. You gotta have all your marbles to stay in the game.

The California Savings and Loan sign flashed seventy-five degrees and 6:05 a.m. when I drove by. Another scorcher on its way. I checked into the Best Western on Fairfax and turned the air conditioning up to high before hitting the sack. Twelve hours later I checked out, much cooler.

•

The final act of the case played a few months later. Wanda called one day to say she was leaving L.A. I stopped by that evening to wish her well.

The U-Haul truck was all packed and the canyon house was bare. Beverly's portrait leaned against a wall in the empty living room.

"Where are you going?" I asked.

"San Francisco. I hear the women are real friendly there."

"You can never have too much of a good thing."

"Are you taking the painting?"

"No. I thought you might want it. You had a real case for her, didn't you?"

So, Beverly, wearing just a Panama hat and very long hair, hangs on my office wall now. And Wanda James visits her ex-lover every couple of months at the California Institute for Women in Fontana.

A Neat Crime

ROSE MILLION HEALEY

"Hello, wiseguy—eh, *Ms.* Wiseperson," Lieutenant Foyle said, entering my office. "Wanna talk murder? I've got one that's a dilly."

Foyle is a walking contradiction in terms: a likeable male chauvinist. For going on twenty years now, the cop and I have maintained a like/hate relationship. Of course, he's never forgiven me for quitting the force and starting my own business. But what really bugs Foyle is that I've managed to keep Ade's Detective Agency afloat without resorting to *Remington Steele* flim-flam. I don't hide behind a fictitious male boss, and if I do say so myself, Ade's has a comfortably high batting average of satisfied customers.

This irks Lieutenant Foyle no end. Whenever he has a chance, he drops by to brag about the latest triumphs of New York's finest. Occasionally, though, he presents me with a teaser, a case that hasn't been solved to the greater glory of the Boys in Blue. Foyle will never admit it, but at those times, he's asking for the help I used to give him when I was a rookie in his squad room.

This, it seemed, was one of those times. Things had been quiet all day, so I was pleased to see the scowling countenance of Lieutenant Francis Y. Foyle. Not that I could let him know it. The motto of our mutual irritation society was: anything you say can, and will, definitely be held against you.

In silence I allowed him to remove his soggy overcoat. Without asking, I poured him a mug of coffee. As he lowered his spare frame onto the chair opposite my desk, I said, "Don't tell me, let me guess. Manda Haley?" I tapped the newspaper I'd been perusing before Foyle's arrival: *Action Demanded in TV Star's Murder*.

The lieutenant grunted. He looked so haggard, my impulse to chortle died aborning. You don't kick a man when he's down, unless you're Mike Hammer.

"According to the *Post*," I said, "the victim didn't lack for enemies. What's the matter, Frank, can't you narrow it down?"

"Sure, sure. Narrow." Slumping back, Foyle closed his eyes. "In the eight days since Haley got blasted, we've eliminated approximately eighty suspects. Everybody hated her. Consequently, everybody stayed away from her. They all have iron-clad alibis. Except. . . ."

I leaned forward. "Except her husband, his light o' love, and 'Mr. Fuss-Budget.' Right?" I was showing off.

Foyle squinted at me balefully. "Who told you?"

"All I know is what I don't read in the papers," I said. "They're the three least mentioned by the media. My nose smells official red herrings."

"You and your nose," Foyle scoffed. "Nobody loves a smart aleck, Thelma."

"But they come to them when all else fails," I said.

Foyle's eyes snapped shut again. "I didn't come to you for anything but commiseration," he said. "This one goes into the Crater/Hoffa bin."

Aware that he'd die rather than confess I might be of assistance, I urged, "Why don't you give me a run-down? I love to hear you tell a story, Uncle Frank."

He grimaced. "The last chapter's missing. And don't flatter yourself that womanly intuition can give it a happy ending."

Foyle had thrown down the gauntlet. There's nothing I enjoy more than a game of One Upmanship with Francis Y. Foyle. "Try me," I challenged.

Well, much of what he had to say I'd already gleaned from TV and newspaper coverage. Manda Haley, who played the hellcat on *Hellgate*, an enormously popular soap opera, would play no more. She had been found dead on the floor of her "sumptuous townhouse" by her maid. The maid had spent Sunday with her parents in New Jersey. She'd discovered the body at ten a.m. on Monday. The medicos put time of death some twelve to fourteen hours prior to that. The "black-satin clad body," incidentally, had been "unviolated," forcing the yellow journalists to abandon their initial "lust-crazed fan" theory.

Manda had been shot by her own platinum-handled .32. Apparently, an attempt had been made to make her death look like a suicide. The gun was found in her hand, but since the bullet had entered squarely between her much-publicized green eyes, there was no doubt about its being murder. The maid reported that nothing had been stolen, ruling out robbery. There having been no forced entry, it was assumed that the actress had let her assailant into the house.

The new information I learned from Foyle's droning narrative was that the police believed Manda Haley had known her killer well enough to have been drinking with him or her shortly before she died.

"How did you arrive at that conclusion?" I asked.

"A couple of things make it fairly certain," Foyle said. First, the autopsy revealed vodka had been recently consumed. We know Haley didn't go out that evening, because she called a number of people, complaining of being bored and asking them over. No one admits to having accepted the invitation, but we had the maid take inventory of the deceased's bar. The vodka supply was diminished. Not surprising. Haley always stuck to vodka. More significant was a fresh bottle of gin that had been opened and a couple of ounces poured off. According to the maid, her mistress detested gin and only kept it on hand for guests."

"The guest, of course, didn't obligingly leave a glass to be examined?"

Foyle gave me a disgusted look. "Are you kidding? This was a very neat murderer. There were *no* glasses in the living room, not even the dead woman's."

I thought that over. "Shouldn't hers have been there?"

"Yeah, well, we figure the killer forgot which glass was Haley's. Gin and vodka look the same."

"I suppose all of your three suspects drink gin?"

"They've been known to do so, bright girl," Foyle said. "And before you suppose about the gin bottle, only the victim's fingerprints were on it. Apparently, she did the pouring."

"No prints elsewhere?"

"Baby it's cold outside," Foyle said to me. "Anyone could have worn gloves when coming to call. Haley wouldn't have thought that was odd. And, of course, if there was time enough to try a suicide cover-up, there was time enough to wipe clean anything that had been handled without gloves."

"I assume something important had been wiped clean?"

Foyle regarded me with a mixture of pride and disdain. He thinks he taught me everything I know, but that it isn't much.

"Cute, aren't you?" he said. "You zeroed in on what we thought was our one lead. The ash trays. In the living room they were empty and clean as the well-known whistle. But only in the living room. All over the rest of the house, the ash trays were loaded with butts from those long Egyptian numbers the deceased smoked. Boy, she was a slobby dame. Her maid goes away for one day, and the place is a mess. You should have seen the kitchen! Dirty dishes piled higher than Amarillo Slim's chips. Going through that garbage pail was no picnic, believe me." He shuddered.

"You checked it for the killer's cigarette leavings?"

"Sure, we did," Foyle growled. "We tore the place apart. Think we're amateurs? There weren't any cigarette leavings."

"Either the killer didn't smoke, or Manda and her visitor never got around to lighting up that evening," I said.

"That's unlikely. Haley was a chain smoker. My three candidates haven't heeded the Surgeon General, either. They all smoke. I thought we could pin down who'd been there by the butts." He sighed. "I could have saved a lot of trouble if I'd known before I went garbage collecting that all three smoke the same brand." Shaking his head, he moaned, "How's that for luck? All three of 'em."

"Fill me in on your Unholy Trio," I said, hoping to divert him from melancholia.

Calming himself, Foyle settled back and treetopped his fingertips. "Peter Merit, actor. Plays the good guy on *Hellgate*. Forty, handsome, if you're partial to silver hair and a Barrymore profile. Immaculately groomed. Quiet, polite, but I think capable of violence if riled. He married Manda Haley three years ago. Says her Lady Macbeth roles were typecasting. She made him so miserable they separated after a few months. At the time, she'd been in favor of a divorce. All he had to do was sign over his eye teeth in exchange. Merit agreed, and as soon as Manda could fit it into her busy schedule, she was going to Reno. Then Merit made his mistake. He fell in love with Lucy Tyler. She's twenty-two, but she passes for a teenager on *Hellgate*.

"I've never seen her on the show." In answer to Foyle's raised eyebrows, I added defensively, "I watch it, if I'm home with a cold or something."

Mercifully, Foyle let that pass with only a sardonic smirk. "Tyler's a high-strung type. Could lose control. She may or may not be the fragile flower she seems. One thing's for sure, she's as crazy about Merit as he is about her. They were dying to get married. Manda Haley was the stumbling block. When she found out about their plans, she turned dog-in-the-manger. For spite, she reneged on the divorce. Women!"

"Men!" I responded automatically. Getting back to the problem at hand, I said, "So the lovers had motives. What about opportunity? Where were they on the murder night?"

Foyle shrugged. "He says he was at the movies. Can't prove it. She claims to have been home alone, studying her script. Tyler and Merit keep separate apartments."

I raised my eyebrows.

"Lucy lives with her *mummy*," Foyle said with emphasis. "A very strict and possessive parent, in case you've wondered why the lovebirds were so hot on making it legal."

I nodded. "If it weren't for mummy, they could just live in what used to be called sin." I thought I had an idea. "What was Mrs. Tyler doing Sunday night?"

Foyle grinned. "Don't worry, we considered her motive: pure daughter wasting her youth waiting around for a married man. Sorry. Mrs. T. couldn't have done it. The old biddy was attending a church supper. Umpteen witnesses. I *told* you, Thelma, everybody has an alibi. Except Peter Merit, Lucy Tyler and Selby Pain-in-the-Neck Hobart."

"The papers labeled him 'Mr. Fuss-Budget,'" I said.

"I could label him, but it'd be unprintable," Foyle grumbled. "What an egomaniac. Made a federal case out of being questioned."

Selby Hobart, I recalled, was a celebrated designer. Celebrated, also, for his feuds, temper and eccentricities. I remembered seeing pictures of him in fashion magazines: stratospherically tall, bald, with a Fu Manchu moustache.

"Hobart's brownstone is next door to the Haley place, isn't it?"

"Right," Foyle said. "World War Three was being waged between the two houses. Hobart and Haley battled about everything. He objected to her stereo, her parties, name it. He sent her anonymous letters, threatening things that would curl your curly locks. She was suing him for harassment."

"He wouldn't kill her over a law suit," I objected.

"With that unstable character, don't be too sure. But there's more. The day before Manda Haley died, Hobart's lawyers tried to effect a settlement out of court. Some settlement! During the meeting, Hobart attempted to strangle his opponent. The lawyers had to drag him off her. She swore she'd have him put in a booby hatch. He swore she wouldn't live to see the day."

"Wow!" I was impressed. "And he has no alibi?"

"Insists he 'resorted to sedatives to calm his shattered nerves' and slept through the night in question."

"That makes him a juicy suspect, all right," I said.

Foyle slammed his palms on his knees. "Hell, they're all juicy suspects. There's just no juicy evidence. If I had a shred—I'd lay odds one of those three did it. But go prove *which* one."

He looked at me hopefully. I wished I could come up with the brilliant inspiration he seemed to expect. . . . Nothing. Stalling for time, I said, "Let's recapitulate. Okay?"

"Awe." He leaned back. "What good will that do? I'm sick of talking."

"Well, maybe it'll sound different if I tell it," I said. Planting my elbows on the desk, I cupped one of my chins in my hands and began: "Once upon a time, a beautiful—witch—got shot by her own gun. . . ." I interrupted myself. "Where'd she keep it, by the by?"

"Her maid said Haley kept it near her when she was alone. She was afraid of intruders."

"I thought so."

"Sure you thought so, after I told you," Foyle jeered.

I ignored that. "So, once upon a time, a lovely, but loathsome lady was spending the evening alone. Suddenly, there comes a rapping on her front door. She peeps out. It's someone she recognizes. Someone she knows has reason to hate her. But she's arrogant, and her loaded thirty-two is easily available. It's a boring Sunday night. She'd enjoy tormenting the poor soul who's come to appeal to that hardened heart of hers. 'Please, drop the lawsuit . . . Please, divorce me . . . Please, set my boyfriend free!'"

Fascinating as your performance is," Foyle said, "it's a re-run."

"Okay, okay. I'm getting to the interesting part," I promised. "Picture the scene in your mind's eye, Frank." Following my own advice, I warmed to the subject. "A luxurious room, the voluptuous siren in black satin. Enter the desperate supplicant. The two of them talk, smoke, drink. Then they argue and *bang!*"

"I know all that. I told you that," Foyle protested.

"Yes," I agreed. "But you didn't elaborate much about afterwards. What the murderer did after the crime might tell us a lot."

"It tells us we're dealing with a cool customer who calmly set about faking a suicide."

"Does it?" I mulled the question over. Something nagged at me. Something Foyle had said earlier didn't jibe with the cold-blooded mopping-up process he'd described. "The killer must have been rattled, Frank. Murder isn't an everyday occurrence in anyone's life. And this crime wasn't premeditated. . . ."

"Well, sure, the weapon wasn't brought into the house, but. . . ."

"It was *there*, grabbed up on the spur-of-the-moment. Maybe even used in self-defense."

"No sign of a struggle," Foyle pointed out.

"That doesn't mean there wasn't one. If glasses were washed and ash trays emptied, the furniture could have been straightened."

"As I said, 'a cool customer.'"

"No one could be cool in that situation," I said. "Suddenly guilty of unintentional murder, anyone would try to cover up. But not coolly. Mistakes would be made. And there's a mistake here. I feel it, but I can't put my finger on it."

"Give your finger a rest," Foyle advised glumly. "We're up against the perfect crime."

We stared at each other. Neither of us had ever uttered the dreaded words "perfect crime." I don't know what my old friend was thinking, but my mind slogged away doggedly, refusing to accept defeat.

In extremus, I sometimes try to fit my size nines into the criminal's shoes. Although Foyle pooh-poohs the idea, identifying with the perpetrator can put a new light on things. We needed all the light we could get.

I concentrated. Let's see. I've shot someone. In a fit of anger or in self-defense. I stand over the body, appalled at what's happened. The first thought would be to run. I rush to the door, then realize I'm leaving behind incriminating evidence. I don't know how much time I have. Someone may have heard the shot. Someone may come. Panic-stricken, I glance around. What have I left? My gloves. My coat. What have I touched in the room?

The gun first. Wipe it with my gloves. Where should I put it? Why not place it in her hand? In a way, she killed herself. I'm not a murderer. I didn't mean to do it. Oh, God, no one will believe that, if they find out I was here. Quick. Quick. Straighten the furniture. What else? Hurry. Hurry. What else might give me away? The ash trays. . . . The glasses. . . . Where to put the cigarette butts? Which glass is mine? . . .

Which glass?

"That's it!" I yelped.

Foyle jumped, roused from his reverie. "What's it?"

"The killer washed *both* glasses."

"Big news," Foyle said sarcastically. "Hell, I thought you had a lead."

"I have. I'm sure I know who killed Manda Haley. Listen, why would a murderer waste valuable time washing both glasses?"

"We've gone over that, Thelma."

"Go over it again," I urged.

"Gin and vodka look the same. The drinks were probably poured into the same kind of glasses. The murderer got confused. He didn't know which glass was which."

"Aha! *He* would know. But *she* wouldn't."

"What?"

"There must have been lipstick on both glasses!"

"That's—yeah." Francis Y. Foyle was on his feet. If he'd been a cartoon, a light bulb would have appeared over his head.

"Frank, lipstick on the cigarettes. . . ."

Francis Y. Foyle snatched up his coat and started toward the door.

"A man," I continued, trotting along behind him, "would have made a mess getting the contents of the ash trays into his pockets. He'd have picked the tell-tale butts out. A woman could dump the whole thing into her purse. Grill Lucy Tyler. If you get the lab boys working on her purse for traces of Egyptian tobacco, I'll bet. . . ." I stopped. I was talking to an empty office.

The next time I saw Francis Y. Foyle, he was a happy man. That morning's headlines had screamed: *Baby-Faced Blonde Confesses*.

"Chalk up another victory for the department," Foyle said. In a gruff voice he added, "Couldn't have done it without you. You're damned good."

Praise at long last. I felt a glow of pleasure.

Then he ruined it. "You know, Thelma," that male chauvinist said, "you think just like a man."

Only a Matter of Time

BEVERLY McGLAMRY

I've never had the least desire to be a detective. Closest I'd come to murder and mayhem was between the pages of a mystery novel, and even then I preferred my corpse laid out neatly on a library rug. I've been Jason Goode's housekeeper (doubling as a cook whenever we're here at his island retreat just off the coast of Florida) for more than a quarter century, and the position suits me right down to the ground. Now mind you, I'd not want to manage one of the businesses which shelter beneath the gilt-edged umbrella known as Goode's Enterprises, nor would I care to be kin to the man. He didn't get to be rich as Croesus by being gentle and kind, and that's the truth! But he demands a well-run home — whether it's his Palm Beach mansion or what he calls his *island shack* — and pays me handsomely to make sure he gets just that.

Or did. Early this morning, someone murdered Jason Goode. Hit him over the head with one of my cast-iron skillets. Which I couldn't help but feel was adding insult to injury, in a manner of speaking.

Still, it wasn't the choice of weapon that set me to playing sleuth, nor even the fact that I'm old fashioned enough to disapprove of killing on principle alone. It was our peculiar situation that was the cause of my taking on the job. We'd had a rip-roaring thunderstorm the night before which, as usual, had knocked out the phones. Since Cap'n Paul had taken the *Mermaid* over to Miami to pick up supplies and wasn't due back for another twenty-four hours, there were six mighty edgy folk stranded on this little island. And one of us was a murderer.

It hadn't been a particularly congenial group to start with, and once they got over the shock of finding Mr. Goode's body, uneasiness and suspicion were quick to set in.

"Annie, I'm terrified!" Senna Goode, her green eyes rounded dramatically, shuddered as she crept into the kitchen. Mr. Goode's fourth wife, she is, and not a day over twenty-five. Although her blonde hair was slightly mussed, her beautiful face showed neither terror nor grief. She hadn't had the decency to change out of her neon-pink pants and matching peek-a-boo top, either, so I found it kind of hard to give her the respectful sympathy a proper widow deserves. "Jason never had locks installed on any of the bedroom doors. I won't sleep a wink tonight, knowing there's a killer in this house!"

Young Mr. Christopher—that's Mr. Goode's son, by his first wife—spoke from the threshold. "I'll move a couple of camp cots into Diane's mother's room," he offered, "and the three of you can barricade the door until morning. It's an inside room, so you'll be secure enough." His voice was quiet, but it seemed to me there was a new authority to it. His father, I think, had always regarded him as rather a wimp—Mr. Christopher's the bookish sort and looks it, horn-rimmed spectacles and all—but I guess knowing you've inherited a fortune puts steel in a man's spine. Or had it been there all along?

Senna shuddered again and gazed appealingly at the tall dark stepson, who was six years older than she was. "I don't dare trust *anyone* until we discover who did this awful thing," she whimpered. "Except you, Chris." She eased forward and stretched out one slim white hand. "Couldn't you spend the night on the chaise in my room?" she begged. "It's the only way I can possibly feel safe."

I set down the pot I was holding with an angry thump. I'd had a notion Senna Goode had been eyeing Mr. Christopher with un-motherly interest, and this proved it.

"But there's Diane to consider," he said slowly, and silently I applauded the turndown that was sure to follow. Diane Pringle was wearing Mr. Chris's diamond, a fact which thrilled her loud-mouthed mother but had caused no end of trouble between Jason Goode and his son. Even though Diane was attractive, in a pixyish kind of way, she came from working-class folk. And Mr. Jason, a self-made man himself, had been something of a snob. Still, even though I privately agreed that Mr. Christopher deserved better than a girl whose only assets were those you could see, I figured he was a lot safer with Diane right now than being preyed on by the far-from-grieving widow!

"You bet there's Diane!" Marsha Pringle, clearly furious, erupted into the room with her embarrassed daughter and her son, Ronald, in tow. The young man's expression was one of complete indifference, his usual reaction to his mother's all-too-frequent displays of temper. Ron had been hired by Mr. Jason a year or so back to do odd jobs around the place and to be caretaker on the island when the Goodes weren't in residence. Employing someone who was trying to kick a drug habit had been cautious philanthropy on Jason Goode's part, and I found myself studying the boy suspiciously. If Ron had gone back to his old ways, and Mr. Jason had learned about it. . . . But that thin-lipped, acne-scarred face told me nothing, so I turned my attention to his mother.

"You'd better not forget there's Diane, neither!" Marsha Pringle was peppering Senna Goode with fresh-milled venom, and her doughy cheeks and jowls were puffed up even further by the bellows of her anger. "She and Chris'll be married come September and it'll be her who's in charge of all this, and not you!" She waved a pudgy bejeweled hand to encompass the sprawling house with its screened patio and pool, the tiny island covered with scrub pine, palmetto and sea grape, and the curving white beach that the afternoon sun decorated with glitter. But I knew she was thinking more about the estate on the mainland and everything it represented.

"Mrs. Pringle, Senna didn't mean to imply. . . ." Chris put in sharply. But Diane's violet eyes fixed beseechingly on his frowning face and he surrendered to her mute pleading. It was those expressive eyes, plus the gleaming cap of baby-fine hair framing delicate features, that had Mr. Christopher so besotted, I expect. Yet I'd often questioned whether Diane was quite as fragile as she appeared.

Senna, however, was not to be distracted by a pair of deep-purple eyes, whatever their expression. Her own green ones narrowed into cat-slits. "And I wouldn't be a bit surprised if it was you who killed my husband, Marsha Pringle," she spat, "to make sure your precious Diane will make it to the altar! Jason was dead set against Chris marrying her, and you knew it."

I winced at her choice of words, but no one else seemed to take any notice.

150

"That wouldn't of stopped ol' Chris," Ron said suddenly, sending a knowing leer in the direction of his brother-in-law to be. "Quite the opposite, hey old buddy?"

Christopher Goode swung around and his jaw tightened visibly. It was only because he'd met Diane through her brother that Mr. Chris had been careful, so far, to walk on eggshells around Ron Pringle. His father's murder had obviously driven him to abandon the pussyfooting.

At this point Diane, who'd never been much of a talker (couldn't compete with her mother, I guess), dissolved into tears. Her sobbing, added to the noisy bickering between Senna Goode and Marsha Pringle, and the heated words being exchanged by Ron and Mr. Christopher, was what set me off. Not a one of them was giving thought to the dead man lying out on the patio alongside the striped canvas chair that had been his particular favorite. And that just wasn't right. Besides, even though Senna was a shallow, self-centered female, she'd said one thing I couldn't quarrel with: How could we feel safe during the night ahead while a person who'd already killed once lay under the same roof?

I picked up the pot I'd used earlier to convey my feelings and brought it down so hard on the countertop that the tile cracked. Then I spoke into the stunned silence. "We're all going into the living room," I said sternly, "and sit ourselves down. One by one, we're going to say where we were, and what we were doing, between the time the boat left just before dawn and seven a.m."

For this was the hour being announced by the brass chronometer on the mantel when I'd walked out to the patio and discovered poor Mr. Jason's body. Like the rest, I'd risen around five, as we generally seemed to do during the hottest part of the summer, and I'd seen with my own eyes that Jason Goode had gone down to the dock to see Cap'n Paul off. Both his son and Ronald Pringle had been with him then. So it only made sense that it was the ninety minutes between sunrise and seven o'clock that mattered here.

Nobody argued, which surprised me considerably. They stared at me and at one another. Diane's tears dried as if by magic; Marsha Pringle shrugged her beefy shoulders; Senna tucked a strand of pale gold hair behind one ear; and the two men, jaws and fists slowly unclenching, just sort of stood there like a pair of toe-scraping schoolboys. Then, as if the lot of them had been kindergarten children, they filed ahead of me into the long room, where a trio of ceiling fans stirred the sultry air that the afternoon sun thrust through west-facing windows. These overlooked what Mr. Jason had been fond of calling his garden. He'd had jacaranda and poinciana trees planted there, and flowering shrubs—hibiscus and alamanda and the like. The riot of color made a fine advertisement for the tropics, but I'd no time now to appreciate it.

I looked across at Mr. Christopher; if he'd go along with me, the others would be forced to. "What did you do this morning," I asked him, "after the boat left?"

He hesitated, and I felt my knees start to shake. I've always had a soft spot for Mr. Chris and had hated it whenever Mr. Jason belittled him. But just suppose the older man had finally said one contemptuous word too many?

"I headed back to the house," he said finally. "I figured you'd have breakfast going, Annie, and thought I'd fix a tray and take it to my room. Last night I fell asleep over an article about marine life on coral reefs, and I planned to finish reading it while I ate."

My heart sank like a stone. I'd been in the kitchen the whole time, and I knew he'd never set foot in there!

"I changed my mind, though," he went on after a moment, "and decided to read for a half hour before I had breakfast. But there was another article that caught my eye while I was flipping the pages—about a sixteenth-century Spanish galleon some divers from the Keys located recently—and the time just slipped away." Apology darkened his myopic eyes. "I was in my room the whole while, Annie, until I heard you scream." He cleared his throat and avoided looking at the young man sprawled in the chair next to his. "But I do know that Ron was still with Father when I left the dock. And that the two of them were arguing."

Ronald Pringle jerked upright, ready for battle once more. "Now hold on! We weren't arguing, exactly. He'd heard from someone"—he flashed a poisonous look at Christopher Goode—"that I'd had some . . . friends come to see me, guys I'd given my word to stay away from. Wasn't true, and I told him so. He believed me, too! When he'd gone"—his heavy-lidded eyes flicked this way and that as if daring anybody to contradict him—"I flopped down on a pile of canvas in the boathouse and went back to sleep. It was barely morning, y'know."

The challenge was promptly accepted. "The place was empty at six-thirty," Senna Goode purred, and I knew she took great delight in naming Ronald a liar. "I happened to glance into the boathouse while I was taking a walk before breakfast. I'd been gathering a few of the blossoms that grow at the edge of the lawn near there"—she gestured vaguely; unlike her late husband, Senna had no interest in native plants—"because they were exactly the same shade as my outfit. I thought they'd look nice in my hair."

Diane made a small sound of protest, then spoke for the first time. "But Senna, the periwinkles are a *pale* pink, almost a nursery pink." Well, I've hinted that there wasn't much behind that pretty face of hers. Here we were with a murder to be solved, and she starts a debate about *posies*, for heaven's sake! Or was she trying to distract us for some reason of her own?

"Not those," Senna retorted impatiently. "The other ones that smell so sweet. Only thing growing on this godforsaken island that has any scent at all, come to that."

Mr. Christopher nodded. "The marvel-of-Peru," he confirmed. "Around here we call them four o'clocks, Diane."

The girl turned a bewildered face to him as if to speak further, but her mother interrupted. "So far as Diane and I are concerned," she said stridently, "we were together during the time you're talking about. You might say we was having a mother-daughter chat." She smiled smugly, but I saw Diane flush scarlet and even though I'd noticed the pair of them going into Diane's room just as the boat's engines revved up, I doubted they'd stayed there very long.

Marsha's voice rasped on, elaborating on the mother-daughter intimacy she was so anxious to promote, but her words were little more than a wasp-drone in my ears. There was a thing that had been said here, within the last few minutes, that was nagging at me.

I looked around at the familiar faces, trying to penetrate the masks of grudging attentiveness or just plain annoyance that each of them put on as garrulous Marsha screeched into high gear. Ron was frankly glowering and paying no heed whatsoever, yet I could have sworn I glimpsed a bit of honest confusion in his eyes as he darted a resentful glance at the woman who'd punctured his alibi. Mr. Christopher seemed torn between heightened suspicions of Ronald and a desire to comfort Diane, who was by now clearly aghast at her mother's exaggeration of the brief conversation that had actually taken place that morning.

Senna Goode, boredom eloquent in the audible sigh that escaped her brightly-painted mouth, shifted deliberately in her wicker chair to face Mr. Chris, who sat on her left. Even in profile, I recognized the slow smile she offered to the object of her concentration when he happened to look in her direction. It was remarkably similar to one she'd given me when she passed through my kitchen at six a.m., headed for that walk she'd told us about. Seeing I was preparing to make pancakes for breakfast, she'd asked me oh-so-charmingly to scramble her an egg instead. "I'll be wearing every bite of your delicious hotcakes on my hips," she'd murmured, posturing so I might have ample opportunity to admire that perfect body of hers. I hadn't answered, except to grab the skillet off the stove and plunk it down on the butcher block beneath the corner window. As the wife of my employer, her wish was my command; but I wasn't about to follow the pattern of certain mornings in the past and put myself out to suit a variety of appetites. I made up my mind they'd all eat scrambled eggs today, and if anyone else came in and started to complain, he'd get mighty short shrift from yours truly! As it worked out, though, the problem didn't arise; not another soul did I see up to the moment I went into my room to tidy up and tie on a clean apron, as I invariably do before announcing that a meal is ready.

It can only have been common sense that nudged me to prick up my inner ear then, and darned if it wasn't Diane Pringle's scatter-brained remark that popped into my head to make me examine more closely the scene I'd been idly reviewing. Blending these morsels of memory resulted in an unlikely pudding that was nonetheless tempting me to dig in. So I tasted it, gingerly at first, and was downright thunderstruck to realize that my meandering thoughts had presented me with the identity of our murderer!

"Ms. Senna, what did you do with those flowers you picked?" I asked, slicing right through the last sentence of Marsha Pringle's marathon monologue.

She spread her hands and widened her eyes. "Why, when you screamed, you scared me so that I dropped them, Annie. I was on the pier at the time and they tumbled into the water. I was so frightened I couldn't even move, and my sweet bouquet floated clear out to sea before I was able to make myself run up to the house." She lowered her lashes and looked sideways at Mr. Christopher. "And I think I'd have fainted on the spot, Chris, when I learned what had happened, if you hadn't been there for me to lean on."

No doubt the seductiveness in her soft voice was genuine enough, I thought grimly. But the innocence she was trying to project was as skimpy as the disgraceful beach outfit she had on.

"Those pink flowers," I said so harshly that everyone's head jerked toward the spot where I stood, "are nicknamed *four o'clocks* 'cause that's the time they open each day. Until late afternoon, you hardly notice them. And they give off no perfume at all."

The color drained from Senna's face, and most of her beauty with it.

"You were never picking four o'clocks just after sunrise," I went on tightly. "And you were the only one who knew I had the iron skillet sitting on the chopping block. I expect my habit of banging pots and pans around when I'm upset reminded you of how heavy it is, and what a fine weapon it'd make for a woman who was scheming to replace an aging husband with a young one"—I ignored the startled exclamation that told me Chris Goode had caught on at last—"and still keep hold of the luxuries she doesn't fancy doing without! You knew well enough where to find Mr. Jason, too. Like me, you've seen him go day after day to sit by himself on the patio so's he might enjoy the cool and quiet of early morning. All you had to do was wait 'til I'd finished cooking and gone to freshen up, when there'd be nothing and nobody to stand in your way.

"You raised such a fuss about being murdered in your bed," I finished, as a horrified Mr. Christopher sprang to his feet, and the chronometer's measured chimes named both the hour and the pink-petaled flower that had pointed the finger of guilt at a killer. "Well, you're not likely to die there tonight. Not unless you're intending to commit suicide, Senna Goode!"

The Best Bid

CAROL COSTA

Dana sensed their anger even before she saw their faces. Their foot-steps were deliberate and heavy despite the carpeted hallway between her office and the newsroom. The phone call that preceded their visit had been brief and uninformative.

"We need your help. Can you see us today?" The man spoke in a low voice as if he were afraid his call was being monitored.

"I'm free this afternoon around two," Dana answered. "Can you tell me what this is about?"

"Not on the phone. We'll be there at two."

"Two o'clock right on the button," Dana said, standing to greet the three men who filed silently into her office. "Have a seat."

Dana wouldn't need to ask what line of work they were in. Their clothes made business cards unnecessary: colored T-shirts under long-sleeved plaid flannels hung loosely over jeans spattered with paint, plaster, and the grime of the city. Steel-toed work boots that bore the same elements as the jeans left a dusty trail of footprints across the dark beige carpeting and made Dana regret her invitation to sit down in her newly-upholstered chairs.

"Like I told you on the phone. We need your help. We heard you could do a quiet investigation for us." The spokesman for the group was a bearded stocky man.

"And what would you like me to investigate?" Dana asked.

"This!" The one word reply came from between the clenched

tobacco-stained teeth of the tallest man in the group and was accompanied by the thud of a folded newspaper which he threw on Dana's desk.

A small article on the front page was circled in red: "Civic center contract awarded to Harrison Construction." The article went on to describe the $200,000 project to remodel the offices of city hall.

Dana skimmed the report and then turned her attention back to the burly trio. The third member, who was at least clean-shaven, cleared his throat and spoke in a surprisingly soft voice.

"Miss Sloan, as you can tell, we're all pretty upset. By the way, I'm George Connors, Connors Construction Company, and this is Emil Damiani." The bearded man nodded at Dana. "And Louie Perkins." At the sound of his name, Perkins grunted an acknowledgment. "For the past two years, we've all been bidding on various city projects, and for the past two years. . . ."

"We've been getting the scraps," Louie yelled, jumping to his feet. "While this punk Harrison gets all the gravy jobs. Now we want to know why." He slammed a huge calloused hand across the desk.

"Take it easy, Lou," George Connors said in the same mellow tone. Perkins mumbled an apology and returned to his seat.

"Time after time, we submit good bids, cutting our costs to the bone, only to get beat out by Harrison." Emil shook his head. "He's got to be paying someone off."

"I see," Dana said slowly. "That's a pretty serious allegation. Do you have any evidence of graft?"

"If we did, we wouldn't need you!" Louie bellowed, impatient with the attractive young investigator. "I don't see how this . . . this *girl* is going to help us," Louie told his companions.

Dana looked into Louie's faded hazel eyes, reading the fear and desperation he was trying to hide with his angry outbursts.

"All right, gentlemen, I'll look into the matter and get back to you," she told them. "Frankly, I think you're wrong. But perhaps I can find out enough about the bidding process to put your suspicions at rest and help you succeed with future bids."

"What if we're right about Harrison?" Emil asked.

"If you're right, he and the building commissioner will find themselves on the front page of this newspaper."

"That's good." Lou stood up.

"That's why we came to you for help," George explained quickly. "The *Globe* has always fought for the little guy and you, well, I've followed your career for a long time, and I think you're one hell of a gal." He smiled, a little embarrassed at voicing his admiration for her in front of the others.

"Thank you." Now it was Dana's turn to feel embarrassed. Although she knew she should be used to her public image by now, it still made her feel uncomfortable to be reminded of it.

Five years ago, Dana was a cub reporter who fought off tremors of panic every time the city editor gave her an assignment, but her determination to get the whole story—the true story—had earned her this plush, though small, office, as well as the title of investigative reporter.

Dana no longer wrote her own copy. She had a secretary who took the facts and evidence that Dana provided and strung them into hard-hitting front-page features.

During the last two years, Dana had gone undercover a number of times. Her investigations helped to solve a brutal murder, break up a drug ring operating out of the county nursing home, and save an innocent man from prison. In between, there had been the small, less newsworthy cases involving everything from missing persons to fraud at the supermarket.

Now, she had two full-time assistants and there was never a lack of work. Dana seemed to thrive on the mystery and excitement of it all.

"We just want to set the record straight," Emil said, with the first hint of a smile.

"That's my motto." Dana extended her hand and each of the men shook it in turn. Their initial anger was now defused and Dana saw relief mirrored in the three rugged faces. They left her office, depositing more of the city's dust into the carpeting.

●

It didn't take much research to find that her clients were right about Gary Harrison's construction company getting the majority of the good contracts. The next step was to find out exactly how the bids were handled and the contracts awarded.

The next morning, dressed in a pair of tight-fitting jeans, a sweatshirt, and a battered denim jacket, Dana presented herself at the building commissioner's office. Her light brown curls were pulled back from her face and fastened with a rubber band. She carried a clipboard and pencil. Dana hoped she looked like the average contractor's field assistant.

"Hi," Dana called out to a girl sitting in front of a computer screen filled with numbers. "Could you give me some information, please?"

Reluctantly, the girl got up and walked over to the counter. "What do you need?" Her tone was bored, unfriendly.

"My boss sent me over to get whatever he'll need to present a bid."

"The bids on the remodeling job closed several days ago. And as of now, there's nothing on the boards." She pointed to a bulletin board outside the office in the hallway.

"That's okay," Dana smiled innocently. "We just want to be prepared for when the next project comes up, so can you give me the forms and explain exactly what I have to do? I'd really appreciate it." Dana lowered her voice to a confidential tone. "I just started working for this guy, and I don't have the slightest idea how any of this works."

"You've got to be kidding." The girl's voice was harsh. "I don't have time to conduct a lesson here. I'll give you a packet, but you'll have to figure it out for yourself."

"Hey," Dana raised her voice above the clerk's. "I was under the impression that all contractors, no matter how small, got a fair shake around here. All I want is a little information."

Instantly, a white-haired woman appeared in the doorway of one of several offices behind the counter and reception area.

"What seems to be the trouble here?" she asked the clerk, who now wore the subdued look of a teenager caught cheating on a math exam.

"Nothing, Mrs. Powers," the girl insisted.

"Nothing, my Aunt Susie," Dana shouted indignantly. "I need some help here, and she doesn't want to give it to me."

"Look," the clerk said defensively, "the information is all in the packets." She shoved a bulky envelope toward Dana.

Just then a man entered the office and Mrs. Powers decided to intervene. "Why don't you come into my office, miss, and we'll go over the forms, and I'll answer any questions you might have."

Mrs. Powers opened a gate at the far end of the counter and motioned for Dana to follow her. "I'll have a word with you later, Janine," Mrs. Powers told her clerk in an icy voice.

"Gee, I'm sorry to be a problem," Dana said as she was seated across a large mahogany desk from Mrs. Powers.

The middle-aged woman assured Dana that it was no trouble at all and began explaining the bidding process, step by step.

Dana took notes on her clipboard and, at the same time, observed the woman who instructed her. Grace Powers was a very attractive woman. Her hair was curled softly around a heart-shaped face and her eyes sparkled like huge sapphires, even behind the tinted glasses she wore. The office was as well kept as the woman. The uncluttered desk held only one personal item—a photograph of the petite Mrs. Powers standing next to a young husky sailor.

"The specifications for each job that is put out for bids are programmed into our computer. They are, of course, determined by the city building codes and fire laws. When the bids come in they are checked for accuracy. Some contractors are very poor at simple addition. If an error is found, the bid is returned to the contractor and he is disqualified."

"That seems rather harsh," Dana commented.

"Perhaps, but competition for these city contracts is so keen, we feel that only those who take the time to submit an accurate bid can be considered."

"I hope my boss has a good adding machine," Dana said, eliciting a smile from Mrs. Powers.

"The remaining bids are then fed into the computer and the contractors receive a print-out of their bids, which they then check for accuracy. They have ten days to report discrepancies to this office. So far, we've had no reports.

"On the eleventh day, the computer is activated and it analyzes each bid, comparing it with the building specifications, and decides who will be awarded the contract."

"You're kidding?" Dana was honestly surprised. "Are you telling me that the computer decides who gets the job?"

"That's right. It's totally fair, since a computer is not capable of showing favoritism, or making errors in judgment."

"What about the guys who don't get the job? Do you give them any information about why they lost out?"

"Oh, definitely," Mrs. Powers smiled again, revealing small white teeth. "They receive a print-out of the computer's analysis of their bids."

On the way back to her office, Dana practiced the speech she was going to give to the disgruntled contractors. How could they waste her time like this? A computer couldn't be bribed, and they hadn't even bothered to tell her about the computer print-outs they were getting. It was all down in black and white for them. What more could they ask for?

"Nice outfit." The comment came from Dana's secretary, Marianne, in response to Dana's greeting. Dana paused long enough to ask the whereabouts of her assistants and to take the stack of mail Marianne held out to her.

Throwing the mail on her desk, Dana went into the bathroom and changed into a conservative white blouse and navy skirt, then brushed her hair out and applied some makeup. Presto! The contractor's assistant was transformed into the fashionable newswoman.

Seated at her desk, Dana was about to dial the number George Connors had left and summon the three contractors to her office for a good tongue lashing, when a letter sitting on top of her stack of mail captured her attention. It was stamped special delivery.

"Dear Miss Sloan," it began. "I know that you imagine yourself a champion of truth and justice, a female Clark Kent, pledged to save this city from con men and criminals. Please be advised that I do not fall into either category. Sources tell me that you are investigating the fact that I have received several of the city's construction contracts. There is no way I could fix those bids unless I had a girlfriend working in the commissioner's office, which I don't. End of investigation! If you continue with this stupid inquiry into my business affairs, I will sue you and your newspaper. I value my reputation and will not have it smeared by the three stooges who hired you." It was signed "Gary Harrison" in scribbled, but legible, handwriting.

Dana re-read the letter several times, her anger rising inside her like a pot of water about to boil. "A female Clark Kent, huh?" she said aloud. "Well, Mr. Harrison is about to see Superwoman in action."

The letterhead contained Harrison's phone number and Dana dialed it with trembling fingers, then composed herself and spoke in a cool businesslike voice to the man who answered.

"Mr. Gary Harrison, please."

"Sorry, he's gone for the day. March of Dimes charity auction."

"Pardon me?"

"You know, that shindig at the Hilton Hotel. Gary's one of the 'eligible bachelors' they're dangling in front of those love-starved females. I figure he should bring in at least a dollar ninety-eight." The rough voice laughed at his own joke, and Dana impatiently hung up on him.

Marianne knew all about the auction that Harrison's man was talking about.

"The March of Dimes rounds up the city's most eligible bachelors and auctions off a date with them. All my girlfriends are there with their checkbooks. The proceeds go to the children's hospital. There was a big write-up about it in our paper. I can't believe you didn't see it."

"Can you bring it to me?" Dana asked.

Within five minutes, Dana was in her car heading toward the Hilton Hotel. The newspaper beside her on the front seat was folded over and Gary Harrison's attractive face smiled up at her. Each bachelor was to provide a weekend's entertainment as part of the deal, and Dana was determined to be the woman Gary tried to entertain.

The auction was half over by the time Dana arrived but luck was on her side. She spotted Harrison sitting on the stage, waiting for his turn on the auction block. The newspaper picture didn't do him justice, Dana decided. The camera hadn't been able to catch the lean hardness of his muscular frame, the way he brushed the dark curls away from his forehead with slender nicely shaped hands, or his dancing blue eyes.

There were a few reporters there who Dana knew, so she quickly circulated among them, spreading the word that she was undercover on an investigation. Her identity protected, she took a seat to wait for her prey.

Harrison walked to center stage and was introduced by the master of ceremonies before the bidding began. It was fast and furious, but Dana was not hampered by any of the budget restrictions that kept the other women from bidding as high as she did. At that moment, she was willing to pay any price for a date with Harrison, knowing that her paper would pick up the tab.

When the bidding was over, Gary joined a triumphant Dana to pose for the photographers. Dana said nothing, waiting to see if Harrison would recognize her.

"What's your name?" he asked with a perfectly dazzling smile.

"Diane Keaton." The name of her favorite actress was the first thing that popped into Dana's head.

"Diane Keaton? Like the movie star?"

"That's right," Dana replied without a smile. It didn't seem as though Harrison had any idea who she really was, and Dana began to relax. "It says on the auction sheet that you're taking me to a ski resort in Wisconsin."

"Yes. That is, if you like to ski."

"Love to."

"Fine." Gary was beginning to feel a slight edge of discomfort as her piercing brown eyes looked him over like he was a T-bone steak in the butcher's window. "It's a two hour drive, so I figured we could leave at nine tomorrow morning. Is that all right with you?"

"It's perfect." Dana took out a small pad, jotted down her address, and handed it to Harrison. "I'll be ready at nine."

"Hey, wait a minute," Gary reached toward Dana's arm as she turned to leave. "We're supposed to stay here for lunch. It's part of the package."

"Oh, I'm sorry, I can't. I have to get back to work or my boss will fire me. I'll see you tomorrow." Before he could protest further, Dana hurried out of the crowded ballroom.

She spent the rest of the afternoon digging into Harrison's background. A quick search through the newspaper's computer files showed that he had inherited his construction company from his father a number of years earlier, along with a sizable amount of money and property. Before that, he'd graduated from college with a degree in business administration and a minor in computer programming.

Dana wondered how easy it would be for him to use his knowledge of computers to turn the odds in his favor at the building commissioner's office. Maybe he was involved with that snippy clerk, Janine, and she was helping him.

Saturday morning was bleak and snowy, but Gary arrived at Dana's apartment right on time, carrying the morning edition of the *Globe*. Their pictures, along with the rest of the newly-attached couples, were spread across one whole page of the newspaper.

"Everyone else has an article to go with their picture, but you ran off so fast, they only wrote about me." Gary's voice was apologetic.

"That's okay. I had to get back to work or my boss wouldn't let me have the weekend off, and I'd rather die than miss this ski trip."

On the ride to the ski resort, they chatted easily, with Dana asking a lot of questions about Gary's construction business.

"What are you doing, taking a survey?" he laughed. "Most women could care less about the kind of work I do."

"I think it's fascinating, especially since you've been doing so much important work for the city lately. How do you manage to get all those big contracts?"

Gary took his eyes off the road and looked at her curiously, and for a second Dana was afraid she'd gone too far. But then he smiled and answered her question.

"Easy. I submit the best bid."

Dana's training as a news reporter made Gary an easy target. The unsuspecting contractor told her everything about himself.

"I don't have any family to speak of—my parents both died within a year of each other."

"No brothers or sisters?"

"One step-brother, from my father's first marriage, but I haven't seen him for years."

"I come from a large family," Dana commented. "I never really appreciated them until I went out on my own."

"I've been alone for so long, sometimes I forget how to act around people." He paused and smiled at her. "You're nice to talk to, Diane. I'm glad you decided to bid on me."

They arrived at the resort in time for lunch, then each went to their respective rooms to unpack and prepare for an afternoon of skiing.

As Dana finished putting her things away, the telephone on the bedside table rang.

"Hello," Dana said brightly.

"What are you trying to pull, Miss Sloan? We ask you to investigate Harrison, and instead of doing it, you run off for the weekend with the bum. Your picture is spread all over the newspaper. What do you take us for, a bunch of stooges?"

"Who is this?" Now Dana's tone was impatient.

"Lou Perkins, who do you think?"

"Now you listen to me, Mr. Perkins. You asked me to investigate and that's exactly what I'm doing. I'm here undercover, using an assumed name, which you probably blew by asking to speak to Dana Sloan."

"I didn't blow it. I asked for Diane Keaton, a real stupid alias, if you ask me, but that's what was in the paper under your picture. You're not going to fool anyone with a name like that. I'll bet Harrison is wise to you already."

"No, he's not, but he will be, because I'm going to tell him everything and then enjoy the rest of the weekend. Goodbye, Mr. Perkins. Please don't call me again."

Dana slammed down the phone, more angry with herself than with Perkins. She was supposed to be a professional, yet she had let that stupid letter from Harrison get her so upset that she'd . . . wait a minute. . . . She didn't know Harrison all that well yet, but she did know one thing. He was well educated and well bred. He would never have written a letter like that, calling his competitors stooges — the very phrase Perkins just used. Damn it! It must have been *Perkins* who wrote the letter, and she had fallen for it and gone off on this wild goose chase.

Dana rushed down to the lobby and looked around for Gary, but he was nowhere in sight. She went to the desk and asked them to ring his room.

"Miss Keaton, right?" the desk clerk asked.

"Yes."

"Mr. Harrison was trying to call you but your line was busy, so he left a message for you to meet him on the slope. He said to tell you he's taken care of all your ski equipment."

Dana hurried outside and followed the signs directing her to the ski lift that would take her up to the slope, freshly packed with new-fallen snow. The air was cold, but the sky had cleared and the afternoon sun glistened on the snow, making it sparkle with reflected color.

She joined some other people waiting in line for the chairs suspended on heavy cable that passed by, one after another, picking up skiers and depositing them at the top of the slope.

When it was Dana's turn, she deftly jumped onto a seat as it began its slow ascent. At the last second, a heavy-set man pushed in beside her. Despite the ski mask that covered his face she could smell the strong odor of alcohol and quickly turned her head away. The chair lurched forward and they were on their way.

Her co-passenger was so much heavier than Dana that the chair tilted in his direction, and Dana was stuck in an uncomfortable lopsided position.

Deciding to make the best of the situation she turned back toward her companion. "Beautiful day, isn't it?"

"Yeah," came the gruff reply. "And if you want to see more beautiful days, I'd advise you to stay out of things that don't concern you."

His voice was low and menacing and Dana felt a sudden chill that had nothing to do with the weather. "What did you say?" she asked, looking up into the blackness of eyes that seemed to glow like chunks of newly-lit coal.

"You heard me, Dana Sloan. From now on the building commissioner's office is off limits to you, unless you want your pretty face rearranged."

Dana couldn't believe this was happening. The chair was moving slowly toward the top. She looked in front of her and behind her, but the distance between the lift chairs made it useless to scream for help. Her voice would be swallowed up and lost in the brisk open air. She was trapped with this lunatic who had her wedged so tightly in the seat that jumping was impossible.

"This is the only warning you're gonna get," he snarled. "You stay away from Harrison and the whole contract business, understand?"

"Who sent you here, Perkins?" Her question came out as a hoarse whisper.

The man's massive wet gloved hand reached out and grabbed her around the throat. "You got a real scrawny little neck. One good yank and you'd snap like a twig."

"There are people everywhere. You can't get away with this." Dana sounded unconvincing even to her own ears, and her words only caused the great hulk of a man to laugh, spewing more of the putrid smell of stale whiskey into her face.

His grip on her was paralyzing. Dana had the awful feeling that if she moved in any direction he would choke the breath out of her.

"All right. Whatever you say." Dana force herself to speak in a slow normal voice, hoping that she sounded sincere. "I was going to forget the whole thing anyway. I'm just here on a holiday."

Slowly, he moved his hand up from her neck and patted her burning cheeks. "That's a good girl. You're a real pretty thing. I'd much rather screw you than beat you . . . who knows, maybe I'll get to do both." He laughed again.

Dana swallowed hard, fighting back the scream of terror that was rising in her throat. They were getting near the top now, closer to other people, and safety. She held herself perfectly still, forcing her eyes to focus on the snow that moved swiftly beneath her dangling feet.

"Remember, stay out of the commissioner's office," he warned again. "You go near there and I'll know. And I'll be back to take care of you."

The thump of the chair as it reached the top of the slope jolted his hand away from her. He jumped from the seat and took off running. Dana watched him disappear over the side of the slope, too relieved to be rid of him to scream for someone to stop him.

"Hey, what's wrong?" Gary held out his hand to her, his face lined with concern. "You look like you've seen a ghost."

Dana pushed his hand away as she mentally relived her terrifying ride up the slope and tried to figure out who could have arranged it. One of the possibilities was that Harrison had seen through her charade. Why else had he gone on ahead, leaving her to ride the chair lift alone?

"Diane, Diane!" Gary repeated the name several times before Dana realized he was calling to her. She was almost at the snow-crusted brick shelter, a few yards from the edge of the slope.

Gary caught up with her, and she suddenly spun around to face him. "The name is Dana, Dana Sloan, as if you didn't know."

"Huh?" His face registered his surprise. "Dana Sloan, the reporter?"

"That's right."

"I don't get it. Why the phony name?"

Dana debated for a second about whether she should tell him anything, then angrily blurted out the whole story, including the disgusting encounter with the man in the ski mask.

Gary seemed genuinely upset. "I'm sorry. I should never have come on ahead of you." Dana's face remained tight and angry. "Hey, wait a minute. You don't think I had anything to do with that man on the ski lift, do you? As for that letter, anyone could stop by my office and pick up some of my letterhead. We just leave it out in the open. Listen,

167

I had no idea who you were until just now, or that anyone had a reason to investigate me."

"You must have known that your competitors would be upset."

"Sure, I know there's always some hard feelings when a big contract is awarded, but it's all done by computer. Monday morning, I'll take you over there and have Grace or Janine explain how it works."

"You're real chummy with them, aren't you?"

"Only because I spend a lot of time in their office."

"Obviously. Look, a half hour ago I was willing to forget this whole investigation, but now I'm convinced you're getting those contracts illegally. If you weren't, I wouldn't have been threatened. Someone in the commissioner's office is afraid of being found out and that person sent that goon to scare me off."

Gary protested his innocence but Dana didn't believe him. He *had* to be in on it, otherwise there would be no reason to throw all the good contracts his way.

Dana left the contractor standing on the slope. Returning to the hotel, she repacked her things and took a bus back to the city. She sat next to the window and let the events of the last two days roll over and over in her mind. By the end of the ride, she was pretty sure she had figured out how the bids were being manipulated. Now all she had to do was find out who was doing it.

When her editor heard Dana's story, he called the county attorney, who questioned Dana thoroughly, then arranged for a warrant to be drawn up for the commissioner's records. As a precaution, he also ordered police protection for Dana.

Feeling secure with a bodyguard at her side, Dana called on Lou Perkins at his home. Dana's persistent questions forced Perkins to admit taking Harrison's stationery, as well as writing the letter. But he denied knowing anything about the man in the ski mask.

"I just didn't think you'd really do anything for us, so I sent the letter. I wanted to get you mad. Action springs from anger, you know."

"Yes, I know, but it's not always the right action," Dana replied ruefully.

On Monday morning, the county attorney conducted a quick but thorough examination of the building commissioner's records and found that Dana's theory about how Gary Harrison received the best contracts was correct.

The bids themselves could not be tampered with, since the contractors were checking the computer print-outs against their original submissions. But no one was double checking the building specifications that were being fed into the computer. It didn't take long to discover that the original specifications were being altered so that Harrison's bid would receive the best analysis by the computer. It was a clever scheme. Once Harrison was awarded the contract, he was given the correct blueprints and specifications for the project, which enabled him to complete the job without a hitch.

Commissioner Fontane, his staff, and Gary Harrison were all under suspicion. The office was temporarily shut down so that a full-scale investigation could be launched by the county attorney. The rumors of graft at city hall spread quickly, and the news media gathered outside the commissioner's office, hungry for more details.

Dana said goodbye to her bodyguard and returned to the *Globe* to write her story. Marianne was typing the final draft when Dana had an unexpected visitor.

"Grace Powers is missing," Gary Harrison announced, throwing himself into a chair.

Dana wasn't sure if she was more surprised by his presence or by his statement. Gary didn't give her time to dwell on it.

"Obviously, she's the one who has been tampering with the bids. Why would a woman I thought was a friend try to ruin me?" There was no animosity in his voice, only bewilderment.

"Ruin you?"

"That's right. I'm finished in this town. No one is going to believe I wasn't paying her off."

"You said she was missing. That doesn't automatically make her guilty."

"The commissioner and the county attorney think it does, but they're probably not going to look too hard for her. Why should they? They've got their scapegoat—me."

"I'm sorry." The words sounded automatic and insincere, but for some vague reason, Dana did feel a sudden surge of compassion for the contractor she had helped to discredit.

"You've got to help me."

"Help you?" Dana was suddenly feeling like a parrot, repeating key phrases that Gary uttered.

"Yes. You got me into this mess by masquerading as Diane Keaton, my generous charity-minded date. You must think I'm a total fool." Dana didn't answer, so he continued. "Well, you're right, I am, but I'm not dishonest. I accepted those city contracts in good faith. I had no idea I was getting them illegally."

"No one is going to believe that, either," Dana replied, but even as she spoke, she realized that she believed him. The same vague reason that prompted her sympathy a few minutes earlier was becoming a nagging voice that was protesting Gary's innocence. Perhaps this whole thing was a set-up to make Harrison look bad, just like the letter Perkins sent to her.

Marianne was instructed to hold the story about the city hall scandal until Dana could pay another visit to the commissioner's office.

"I'd like to look at Grace Powers's personnel file," Dana told the county attorney's investigator, who was still in the office. The man shrugged and motioned Dana toward Commissioner Fontane, who was barely visible behind a stack of record books that he and a silent Janine were going over with the investigator.

The commissioner seemed happy for the interruption and led Dana back to his private office, where he handed over Grace Powers's file.

"You can't take it out of my office. They'll want it for the investigation." Dana nodded as Fontane tugged at his face with nervous pudgy fingers. "What a mess. I would never have believed it. Grace has been with me for two years."

"And, coincidentally, that's how long Gary Harrison has been getting the top city contracts." Dana's observation caused the distraught commissioner to shake his head vigorously. "When did Mrs. Powers disappear? She was here this morning when we first checked your records."

"I don't know. I was so upset over the findings. One minute Grace was in her office and the next she was gone. One of the investigators went to check her house. There's not a trace of her left in her office. It's like she was never there."

Dana remembered sitting across the desk from Mrs. Powers and thinking that her office was unusually devoid of personal items.

"When I was here the other day, I noticed a photograph on her desk. Do you know who the young man in the sailor uniform was?"

"Her son, Eric. She talked about him all the time. Sounded like a bum to me, but Grace's whole world seemed to revolve around that kid."

Dana nodded and turned her attention to the personnel file. Commissioner Fontane left her alone to study it. As she hoped it would, the file answered several questions for Dana. Grace was a widow with one son, Eric. Before coming to the Midwest, Grace had been employed by a large corporation in San Diego where she had been in charge of computer operations. She had worked there for twenty-two years. How odd, Dana thought, that Grace would leave a job after that length of time and move from a warm climate to a cold one. Most people did just the opposite. There had to be a reason.

Armed with the phone number of Grace's former employer, Dana quickly left the commissioner's office and headed for an out-of-the-way phone booth where she could make a private call.

When her call to California was completed, Dana had learned the motive for Grace Powers's actions over the last few years. To confirm her suspicions, Dana placed two more phone calls. Emil Damiani and George Connors gave identical answers to the questions Dana asked them.

The last call she made was to Gary Harrison. "Meet me at Perkins's construction yard in a half hour," she instructed.

"Why?"

"Because Mr. Perkins is going to help us set the record straight."

When Dana arrived at the construction yard, Gary was waiting for her and Lou Perkins was trying to throw his young competitor off his property.

"Hold it, Perkins," Dana shouted as she emerged from her car. "He's here with me."

"Then you can get the hell out of here, too," Perkins yelled back.

"Okay I'll leave," Dana replied cheerfully, "but I'll be back with the county attorney."

"For what?" Perkins's voice became shrill, and his stubbled face turned pale.

"To hear the evidence you've been suppressing," Dana said calmly. "Shall we go inside your office and talk?"

Perkins turned and led them to the portable metal building that served as his office.

"I don't know what you're talking about," Perkins said, regaining some of his composure. "I told those other guys we couldn't depend on a publicity-crazed broad like you, but they wouldn't listen to me."

"Oh, but they did listen to you, Lou," Dana replied quietly. "They listened and fell for your story. I just spoke to Emil and George. They both said you came to them and said a reliable source at the commissioner's office told you that Gary was getting the contracts illegally."

Gary suddenly broke his silence. "I don't understand any of this, Perkins. Who gave you this so-called information about me and the bids?"

Perkins just glared at Harrison, so Dana answered the question. "Grace Powers, of course. She convinced Lou that you were cheating him, just like you cheated Eric."

Gary's eyes widened in surprise. "Eric? My step-brother?"

"That's right. Eric is Grace Powers's son. Lou, here, is her brother, and Eric's uncle. I had a long talk with Grace's former employer. He supplied me with her maiden name and told me all about Grace's unhappy life. Apparently, she went to work with him right after she divorced your father."

"So what?" Perkins shouted. "So Grace is my sister. That doesn't prove a thing."

"Tell me, Gary," Dana asked, "when your father died, how much of his estate passed to Eric?"

"Nothing. Everything went to me."

"Why?" This time the question came from Lou Perkins and Gary turned to face him. "Tell me why that bastard cut his first-born off without a cent."

Gary hesitated and shifted uncomfortably before he finally answered. "Eric was overseas. He got caught dealing drugs, and he was dishonorably discharged from the navy. Dad was furious and rewrote his will. He probably would have changed his mind later. Dad was like that. Only he died two weeks after the new will was signed."

Perkins took a deep breath and let it out again. His faded hazel eyes were filled with suspicion. "I never heard about no drugs. You're lying."

"No, Lou," Dana said sharply. "You've been lied to, but not by Gary. Your sister filled you with her lies. She transferred her bitterness and resentment for her ex-husband onto his son. This whole business about the bids was nothing but an elaborate scheme to ruin Gary and avenge the wrong she felt was done to her son. And you helped her."

"I never met Eric's mother," Gary explained, more to himself than to Dana or Perkins. "She used to just send Eric to stay with us during the summer. He was a wild kid, always getting into trouble. I remember when dad found out he was going into the navy he said that was the best place for Eric."

"A wild kid, who grew up to be a surly, drunken man. The same man who accosted me on the ski left yesterday. Another part of Grace's plan to keep me on the case until I uncovered her ingenious method of passing the best contracts to you. Grace wanted everyone to know what she was doing, because she knew they would assume you paid her to do it. Then she slipped away, leaving you to face criminal charges alone."

A defeated Lou Perkins slumped into the chair next to his cluttered desk. "You'll never find her," he said softly. "I don't even know where she went. She set me up too, you know."

"You were her accomplice," Gary shouted, and with a few long strides he was in front of Lou, grabbing him by the shirt collar and pulling him out of the chair.

"Stop it, Gary!" Dana ordered. "Lou is telling the truth. He's a victim of Grace's scheme, just like you are."

"I was just as shocked as anyone when I learned that Grace took off," Lou cried. "That's when I figured she must have been the one tampering with the computer. She told me that skinny girl in the office . . . what's her name?"

"Janine." Dana supplied the necessary information.

"Janine . . . yeah, she told me Janine had the hots for Harrison and that's why she was fixing the bids, and that he was paying her, too."

Gary released Perkins and stepped back, waving his hands in the air in a gesture of frustration. "Great. So we're all victims. What do we do now?"

"Lou is going to come down to the commissioner's office and confess his part in all of this. Then my paper will run the *true* story, and your name will be cleared."

"There will still be those who will choose to believe that Grace and I were partners in all of this," Gary said, matter-of-factly. "I may never get another contract in this town."

"Yes you will," Dana told him firmly. "Today's headlines will be lining garbage cans tomorrow. As soon as a new story hits the front page, this one will be forgotten. That's what keeps me in business."

As Dana predicted, the scandal at the commissioner's office soon faded into obscurity. Grace and Eric remained fugitives, and Lou quietly paid a fine, then left town.

As for Gary, he lost the city hall contract to George Connors, but within a month he was awarded a lucrative state project.

"How do you explain that?" Marianne asked Dana after hearing about Gary's latest good fortune.

"Easy," Dana replied with an innocent smile. "He submitted the best bid."

Contributors' Notes

Elizabeth Burt lives in Eastern Massachusetts, where she works as a newspaper editor and feelance writer. She has published a book on freelance writing and is currently working on a mystery novel featuring a woman reporter.

Helen and **Lorri Carpenter** are a mother/daughter writing team. They are presently working on a longer mystery featuring Emma Twiggs. "The Disappearing Diamond" is their first story to be published in an anthology.

Anna Ashwood-Collins is currently the executive director of the International Association of Crime Writers and a field agent for the U.S. Department of Labor. She lives in Queens, New York, and Jekyll Island, Georgia, and is working on a mystery novel featuring a woman detective.

Carol Costa is an award-winning playwright. Her plays "Death Insurance" and "Big Al Goes Straight" combine the elements of mystery and comedy. She is also the author of numerous radio scripts, short stories and comedy skits.

Ellen Dearmore is a pseudonym. The author of "The Adventure of the Perpetual Husbands" is working on a collection of mystery stories featuring Gertrude Stein and Alice Toklas.

Deborah Hanson, who now lives in Los Angeles, has worked as a magazine writer and editor on both coasts. "The Whisper Business" is her first published short story.

Rose Million Healey has had short stories published in *Cosmopolitan, McCall's* and *Redbook*. Her woman detective, Thelma Ade, was first introduced in *Alfred Hitchcock's Mystery Magazine*. She lives in Manhattan, where she is completing a play.

Gerry Maddren is the author of *The Case of the Johannisberg Riesling* (Cliffhanger Press), forty-four published short stories, and one play. She lives in California and serves on the board of both The Mystery Writers of America (Southern California Chapter), and Women Writers West. She is at work on a novel featuring two women detectives.

Beverly McGlamry lives in South Florida and is a full-time writer. She has had two historical novels published by Ballantine Books and a third novel will be published in Great Britain by W. H. Allen of London.

Nita Penfold received her Master of Arts degree in writing from Lesley College Graduate School in Cambridge, Massachusetts. She is a co-editor for *Earth's Daughters*, a feminist arts periodical published in Buffalo, New York. Her poetry has been widely published, and her fiction has appeared in *Pure Light*.

Judith Post lives in Fort Wayne, Indiana. She is a former elementary school teacher, who now devotes her time to writing mysteries. Her first novel, *Gourmet Killings*, was published by Penny Paper Novels.

Karen Wilson is a technical writer by day and a short story writer by night. She has published several articles and reviews in Los Angeles-area newspapers, as well as in a national magazine.

Other titles in the **WomanSleuth Series**

Murder in the English Department, by Valerie Miner
She Came Too Late, by Mary Wings

The Crossing Press is planning to publish a second volume of contemporary mysteries by women. Short stories featuring women sleuths can be sent to the series editor: Irene Zahava, 307 West State Street, Ithaca, New York 14850. Inquiries about the **WomanSleuth Series** should also be directed to her.